THE DEVIL ON
HORSEBACK

THE DEVIL ON HORSEBACK

Lauran Paine

Thorndike Press • Chivers Press
Thorndike, Maine USA   Bath, Avon, England

This Large Print edition is published by Thorndike Press, USA and by Chivers Press, England.

Published in 1996 in the U.S. by arrangement with Walker Publishing Company, Inc.

Published in 1996 in the U.K. by arrangement with the author.

U.S. Hardcover   0-7862-0519-9   (Western Series Edition)
U.K. Hardcover   0-7451-3921-3   (Chivers Large Print)

Thorndike Large Print ® Western Series.

The text of this Large Print edition is unabridged.
Other aspects of the book may vary from the original edition.

Set in 16 pt. News Plantin by Warren Doersam.

Printed in Great Britain on permanent paper.

British Library Cataloguing in Publication Data available

Library of Congress Cataloging in Publication Data

Paine, Lauran.
      The devil on horseback / Lauran Paine.
         p.   cm.
      ISBN 0-7862-0519-9 (lg. print : hc)
      1. Large type books.   I. Title.
      [PS3566.A34D48   1996]
      813'.54—dc20   95-20827

Contents

Contents

1

Springtime

Winter dies with grudging malevolence: raw, bitter winds and rain squalls. The earth seems torn and swollen, with autumn's dried leaves underfoot. Bare tree limbs of black oaks, creek willows, and cottonwoods are stark silhouettes against menacing skies. Creeks and rivers run brown with erosion's detritus. Villages, towns, and outlying places endure winter's death throes, waiting for springtime and a promise of summer. . . .

Roadways of rutted adobe inhibited all but the most urgent travel. For generations, humankind had lived through the full force of winter with foreshortened activity, shrunken vistas, narrowed concerns, marking time until spring arrived so that work could be resumed; life could at least face an unknowable future with the blessing of warmth and new growth to encourage the only constant of life — hope.

Dirty clouds moved in ragged disarray across a sky of diluted blue. The wind gusted through an ancient Indian ruin known locally as Anasazi Pueblo, at one time extensive and thriving. Now its mud walls had been washed away over the centuries until little remained. Spindly trees grew where roofs had been, gila monsters waddled where bare brown feet had walked. And, it was rumored, *fantasmas* appeared — proof that the Old Ones, the Anasazi, existed beyond sight and touch.

Intermittent squalls of icy rain passed and the trees bent in anguish as a man leaned against a tree, his coat snugged to the throat. His hat was pulled low, his hands covered by gloves. He smoked and watched his thoroughbred-looking bay horse pick grass with little concern for the weather or the wind, which was unusual; horses disliked wind above all kinds of weather. A mud wall, about five feet tall, broke most of the wind's force, which may have contributed to the animal's indifference.

The man had hawkish features with a coppery tint, red-flecked brown eyes that missed nothing, the lean build of a hungry wolf, and the essential requirement for his trade, patience. Great patience.

He was not sure the meeting would be consummated, yet he waited. People were unreliable. Their best intentions diminished, usually because of conscience, a curse in the view of the lean man with the mud-wall windbreak at his back.

During a brief hiatus from the squall, the horse raised its head and turned abruptly with its ears pointing. The lean man ground out his smoke, reset his hat, and stood motionless until he saw the rider appear, vague at first, like one of the *fantasmas* of Anasazi Pueblo, clearer as he came down from the slightly higher mesa, picking his way among old trails, bundled into a sheep-pelt coat that made him appear thicker than he was.

The thoroughbred nickered; the lean man smiled as the rider's head abruptly lifted from watching the trail. Wet mud, especially on a slope and particularly if it was adobe, made treacherous footing.

The lean man stirred, crossed beyond the remains of a mud house where the oncoming horseman could see him, and waited.

The newcomer dismounted stiffly; bitter, bleak weather hardened the marrow in older bones. The lean man noticed and was not surprised. He had already known the man he was here to meet was not young. Otherwise he knew practically nothing about him. The stocky, older man who nodded as he removed his gloves was equally as ignorant about the lean man, but as he studied the bronzed, hawkish face he was satisfied.

They exchanged none of the customary cow-country amenities such as the weather, the price of cattle, the venality of governors and presidents.

The older man's face was flushed from cold, his brown eyes watered from wind. He sighed and shook his head. "It was a long ride. I wasn't sure you'd be here."

The lean man replied in a pleasant voice. "I keep my word, Mister Drake."

The older man looked briefly annoyed. "I'm Mister Smith. What made you figure my name was Drake?"

The lean man showed even white teeth in a wintry smile. "My name is Halcón. Names don't matter." His genial gaze lingered as he held out a hand, palm up. "The money first, Mister Smith, then the name and where I can find him."

Drake had to unbutton his heavy coat to reach the envelope, which he handed to the lean man. "The name is Ed Ballinger. He's the town marshal of Calabasas, west of here about eighteen miles."

Halcón tucked the envelope away and nodded. Before turning toward his horse he said, in Spanish, "Rest tranquil. Good-bye."

Drake watched as Halcón bitted his horse, removed the hobbles, snugged up the cinch, and mounted. The lean man did not look back as he left the cluster of ancient *cuchitriles*. But the older man scowled faintly as he saw him ride due south not due west. For one bad moment Drake scarcely breathed. Three hundred dollars were riding south and if, as his natural turn of mind suggested, Mister Halcón, or whatever-in-hell his name was, decided to keep right on going south there was not a blessed thing Drake could do but regret that he had ever listened to that damned Mexican who had given him Halcón's name and the slip of paper with instructions on how to contact him.

Another of the stinging rain squalls swept through, making eerie sounds among the doorways and windows of the ancient adobe village as Drake swung across leather. Grimacing because he was sitting in water, he headed for that treacherous trail and headed up to the mesa. There he paused for a moment, peering southward, but again the slanting rain obscured his vision. Dark clouds had lowered and the wind gusted, starting low and rising until Drake pulled his head lower inside the sheep-pelt coat as he reined eastward.

It was a long ride. Even in good weather it was tedious as well as uncomfortable for an older individual who was not fond of horsebacking. Drake was a buggy person;

horsebacking was for ranchers, hired hands, and others whose normal pursuits required covering distances and who, in the older man's view, lacked enough good sense to live in towns where money, convenience, the interesting variations of human activity existed.

He had left Calabasas before sunrise, not entirely to reach the ruins on time, but because since he so rarely bundled up for a long horseback ride, people would wonder.

Nor would they wonder as much if he arrived back in town after supper, perhaps closer to midnight when few would be awake.

The wind seemed to be dying, at least it had less force and there were longer intervals between the cold gusts as he headed back without haste. He deplored the necessity for the trip he had made and was not altogether satisfied with the results, but that was part of the nature of Henry Drake. He was not known as a trusting individual.

By the time he reached town he was cold all the way through. As he dismounted in the livery barn's poorly lighted runway, every bone and muscle ached. He was tired, hungry, and exhausted from bracing into winds that rarely came twice from the same direction.

The liveryman's nighthawk was a rail-thin, watery eyed, fumbling, forgetful old soldier named Enos Jordan who wouldn't have been awake in his smelly blanketroll on the harness-room floor if he hadn't been aroused in a cold sweat from a terrifying nightmare that some folks would have attributed to the old soldier's search for a life without torment through the bottom of whiskey bottles.

Jordan heard Henry Drake unsaddling in the runway and remained amid his blankets even when Drake carried his saddle, blanket, and bridle into the harness room to be shoved on the saddle pole. He knew Mister Drake would see him, so he made noises like an old sow until the other man departed, then he sat up, scratched, fished for the bottle, took two swallows, capped it, dropped back, and went to sleep. This time without a nightmare.

Henry Drake used the back alley to reach his building. He lived in a comfortable set of rooms off the back of his mercantile establishment, the only such business within thirty miles in all directions.

He shed his clothing in darkness, climbed between clammy flannel sheets, and composed himself for the sleep that would not come. Worrying people do not sleep well. Those who have just bought a death sleep less well than others.

The town was quiet. It was not large enough to be a town, but it was heading in that direction. When Henry Drake had arrived many years back, Calabasas had been a scraggly community, mostly Mexican, with five saloons, three cantinas over in Mex town, transients passing through in droves, enough commerce to need more, cowmen dominating every phase of local life, and the kind of law one might expect.

The change had been gradual, and grudging, with the arrival of the telegraph, a local stage company office and corralyard, even a medical doctor and a local tannery converted into a hotel where, in especially humid weather, the ancient odors came back despite repeated lye treatment by the proprietor, a transplanted New Englander.

The town's economy had been flourishing for many years now. Calabasas was no longer an ancient town of dust with a predominantly brown color, from the dust to the mud-walled houses, even to the native inhabitants. They still lived apart, had their own stores, watering holes called *cantinas,* and their own community well in the center of the plaza. A circular knee-high wall of adobe bricks prevented children from falling in, but dogs had fallen in, even once a burro.

Henry Drake had watched the growth, had anticipated some of it, and had profited from his foresight. In fact, he had become one of

14

the wealthiest men in the area, which included ranchers whose holdings were in some cases awesome, but in a semidesert country miles of land were required to run any number of cattle.

Henry Drake's driving motivation was money. He cared nothing for prestige, although with wealth prestige was unavoidable. He had a knack for anticipating the needs for land, buildings, capital; had profited from each and every opportunity.

He was in his mid-fifties and had no family, although it was rumored he had abandoned a wife back in Missouri. His territorial acceptance was ambiguous. He would never have won a popular election — nor, as Jim Rourke of the saloon had said, a beauty contest — but his advice was sought and of course there were those who fawned in the face of success. He was a businessman whose clerk at the mercantile rarely sat down in Mister Drake's presence or chewed tobacco in his sight. Henry Drake favored cigars, expensive ones that he did not stock in the store but kept in his office back near the loading dock. His tolerance of those who chewed was low. He would not have stocked such a wide variety of the stuff in the store if he had not known how surly his customers would become if he didn't.

As he lay awake during the small hours, considering the agreement he had consummated at that old Indian ruin east of town, it was not his conscience that bothered him, it was the possibility that he had given three hundred dollars to a man he had never seen before to perform a service. If the lean man failed, not only would Henry Drake be out his money, but the problem that had driven him to hire Halcón would become more acute. If Halcón failed, where could Drake find another man to commit murder?

2

Calabasas

For the Calabasas liveryman the lean, predatory stranger with the big thoroughbred bay was of interest because he was the first customer of the day. In fact the liveryman had only just returned from breakfast at the cafe across from the jailhouse when the stranger rode in, nodded, and dismounted. While the liveryman sucked his teeth and watched, the stranger cared for his animal, stalled him, and as he passed the liveryman to enter the harness room with his outfit, he said, "Good morning. A bait of grain and hay."

The liveryman, a slovenly individual with close-set eyes, a paunch, and large, work-scarred hands, wanted to know if the stranger realized that stalled horses cost a dime a day more than horses turned into a corral.

The stranger hung up his riding outfit before replying. "How much for the grain and hay?"

17

"Another ten cents. How long you figure to be around?"

The bronzed man returned to the runway to consider the liveryman, who was obviously a man of few words with a heart of stone. "Maybe just today, maybe longer." The stranger halted directly in front of the liveryman, his red-flecked brown eyes fixed and unblinking. "Is that all right with you, friend?"

The liveryman stopped sucking his teeth. He thought he knew how a bird felt when it faced a reptile. "Fine with me," he said gruffly, salvaging what he could of his rude attitude.

The weathered man handed over a silver cartwheel and smiled. "We'll settle up when I come back, Mister — ?"

"Jobey, Alex Jobey."

The bronzed, weathered man nodded and walked away.

The liveryman entered his harness room to examine the stranger's outfit. The saddle lacked a maker's name, which was not unusual, and the booted carbine had those sights with a sliding bar for gradient shooting. Neither was that particularly unusual, except that most men used simple buckhorn sights.

The saddlebags contained three flat tins of sardines, a mainstay for men who did not expect to be near a cafe or a supper table. Otherwise there were two boxes of bullets, copper clads for both a .45 Colt and a .30-caliber carbine.

There was a change of clothing, a pigging string, and two sacks of Bull Durham.

The liveryman sat down at his old desk in a chair that creaked under his weight, exhaled loudly, and tried to define exactly what it was about the stranger that had made him uncomfortable.

The cafeman was tapering off after feeding half the town's bachelors and paid little attention to the stranger who asked for eggs, bacon, spuds, and hot coffee. It was the usual fare of rangemen and townsmen, except townsmen usually asked for toast.

Later, up at the saloon, Jim Rourke was washing glasses in oily water when the stranger walked in. Jim hooked the little towel under his waistband and nodded as the stranger, his first customer of the day, leaned on the counter and asked for beer with a jolt in it.

Rourke was a bullnecked, scanty-haired individual in his late fifties who had been in the saloon business since his teens. He had learned it from his father, a native of County Cork and a man of considerable geniality, which was not always his son's attitude.

As Rourke set up the boilermaker he looked straight at the stranger. Calabasas had its share of drinkers, but only one or two who drank doctored beer at seven o'clock in the morning. Rourke asked the time-honored question, "Traveling through are you?"

The bronzed man half drained his glass before answering. "Going north. I'd like to be one of the first to get hired so I struck out early."

Rourke nodded. "The weather ain't helpin' though, is it?"

"No, but I'm used to it. The only thing I never liked was wind. A man can get warm by lighting a fire, he can get cool by finding a creek, but wind . . ."

"For a damned fact," Rourke said. "Even in town a man worries about his roof gettin' torn loose."

"Nice town," the bronzed man said, reaching to finish off his beer.

Rourke nodded. "I've been in lots worse."

"Orderly too, is it?"

Rourke smiled broadly — he and the town marshal had been close friends for years. "We got a lawman that can cull wildcats bare-handed."

"That's the kind it takes, Mister — ?"

"Jim Rourke. To my pa it was O'Rourke,

but I dropped the O."

"I once knew a town marshal named Ezra Benson who was like your man. He kept order in a border town, which wasn't always easy. Sounds like you got another Ezra Benson."

"Maybe, except that our marshal's name is Ed Ballinger." Jim Rourke made a sweep of his bar, lifted the stranger's glass, and swabbed under it too.

"Ezra Benson organized a posse down along the border that'd be ready to ride in fifteen minutes. When they went after someone, they caught him. Does Calabasas have a vigilance committee, too?" the stranger asked.

"Well, not organized ready to ride, exactly, but when Ed calls for riders, we go with him. Most of us, anyway."

"You got a doctor too," said the stranger. "I saw his sign on a little picket fence when I rode into town."

"Oh yeah, we got a doctor, a preacher, law an' order. Calabasas is — An' we got an old screwt who runs the mercantile, name of Henry Drake, who's into everything, owns half the town, is daddy to a bank he says we need."

The bronzed man leaned. "You don't sound like you're real fond of Mister Drake."

"Some folks like him, I guess. I'm not one of them. I can get along with him all right,

21

don't make no mistake about that. He's just one of those money-grubbin' sons of bitches it's hard to like."

The stranger asked how good the hotel was and Rourke replied candidly, "It used to be a tan-yard. When summer's warm rains come, the stink returns. This time of year it's all right. Better to have any kind of roof over a man's head than none at all, eh?"

The stranger laughed, dropped silver atop the bar, and departed. Jim Rourke picked up the coins, thinking his first customer of the day was a likable, soft-spoken, maybe part Mexican individual, not real dark but sure as hell with some variety of blood in him that gave him that faintly coppery look. Jim Rourke had seen them all sometime during his fifty years: skin tones ranging from very pale to just plain pale, and from there up along the spectrum.

The stranger went down to the mercantile, bought a sack of tobacco with wheat straw papers, and went out front to roll a smoke.

Across the road and northward a short distance was the jailhouse. It had adobe walls three feet thick, little barred slits for windows, and an ancient oaken door created by a very talented individual who had reinforced it with steel and large iron bolts. It could withstand a siege.

The building more nearly resembled a fort than a jail. In fact, during Mexico's sovereignty throughout the southwest, the Calabasas jailhouse had been a *cuerpo de guardia,* a military jail. But that had been long ago, almost three-quarters of a century earlier. Now the Calabasas jail, referred to in Mex town as the *juzgado,* was only intermittently occupied. Those thick walls ensured that the little building would be cool in summer and warm in winter, which had something to do with friendly visits a number of townsmen paid to Marshal Ballinger. Another reason was that big Ed Ballinger, in his mid-forties, was a genial man who used force — very well when he used it — only under specific circumstances.

The watcher in front of the general store saw men pass through the open door of the *juzgado*. From their appearance and numbers he suspected the town marshal was widely liked, which was true.

He also suspected that Marshall Ballinger had other interests beside maintaining order; at least three of his visitors were stockmen, faded in looks but with clear signs of affluence such as hand-carved saddles, silver on their spurs, bits, and belts, and in general, the unworried look of men who really did not have to worry.

He had a long wait to identify the lawman. Ballinger emerged eventually with two friends and crossed to the cafe. Ballinger was the largest of the trio, with a badge on his shirt.

He was graying, had a pleasant face with large but not coarse features, and was clearly a strong, healthy individual. He wore his holstered Colt loose, with the tie-down thong hanging free.

After the marshal had passed, the loafer under Henry Drake's plankwalk overhang killed his smoke and turned.

Drake was standing in the store doorway, expressionless. The stranger looked through him as he walked away. There was no slight nod, no faint smile, no words.

Down at the smithy a bald, burly man was nailing a shoe on the hind foot of a twelve-hundred-pound harness animal that belonged up at the corralyard. He looked up, saw the stranger regarding him, ducked his head, and spoke a greeting around several nails in his mouth.

The stranger moved into the shade and said he would like to have new shoes all around on his horse if the blacksmith had time. But there was no hurry; one of these days maybe.

The smith finished nailing, clipped the extruding points, let the hoof down slowly, and just as slowly straightened up. Horseshoeing ruined more backs than a man could shake a stick at, and Slade Downing, the local smith, was only in his thirties. Straightening up would become increasingly difficult and uncomfortable as the years passed.

The smith told the stranger he would make time to shoe his horse whenever the stranger was ready. Right now he was busy, but he could always make room for one more shoeing job. He tightened his apron and was preparing to go around to the other rear hoof when the stranger said, "Hot, hard work, blacksmithing."

Slade Downing could agree with that. He gave a rueful smile. "For a damned fact, friend, but every man's got to serve the Lord whatever he's best at." Slade considered some tapered nails in his hand. "With summer comin' it gets awful hot in here with the forge goin' most of the day."

The stranger was understanding. "Running a forge never bothered me."

Slade's interest in the stranger heightened. "You been a blacksmith?"

"Well, I've pumped a lot of bellows, friend. I never shod a lot of horses. My specialty was forge work."

"In summer?"

"All year around."

"The heat didn't bother you?"

25

The lean man smiled slightly. "No. After a while you get used to it."

Slade Downing snorted. "Not me. Inside this shed at the height of summer it gets as hot as the hubs of hell. I sweat out water as fast as I drink it."

The stranger changed the subject. "When I'm ready I'll bring my horse over."

Slade appreciated that. He would have gone after the animal himself, but if he didn't have to walk over there and lead the horse back it would save time, and today he had work lined up until supper time. "That'd be right decent of you, friend."

As the stranger headed for the livery barn the bullnecked blacksmith looked after him. Now there was the kind of man it was a pleasure to shoe for. Considerate and all.

He went around to the off hoof of the dozing harness horse and went to work. But no one in their right mind did not object to running a forge to white-hot heat in midsummer when the temperature outside was hot enough to fry eggs on a rock; working a forge inside a building got so hot that men had been known to faint dead away from the heat.

The stranger did not return, but Slade had not really expected him to; he had said "someday" and "maybe." Later he saw the stranger leaving Jobey's barn, riding north, and called to him. "Mister, that horse could outrun lightning by the looks of him."

The bronzed man smiled. "He can run if he has to."

Slade Downing's eyes narrowed. "We get up races now an' again. Some of the stockmen around the country think they got fast horses."

The stranger smiled and gently shook his head. "I never race him. He doesn't need the exercise and the money don't mean much to me."

"But, just once. I could bet all I got an' when he won I could set back for a few months."

The stranger showed Slade a genial smile as he shook his head and continued northward. The blacksmith stood with both hands on his hips, thinking that there was never a man born who owned a real running horse who didn't want to get rich off him.

There was no wind for a change but neither was there much heat from the sun, so the big iron stove at the mercantile was popping; someone had just fed dry cedar into it.

The clerk, a youngish washed-out individual of nondescript appearance, came over to wait on the stranger. As the customer named the supplies he wanted, the clerk wrote them on a slip of paper that he took with him as he went among the shelves.

It was not a lot, about all a man with saddlebags would want. The clerk added up the total; the stranger paid it, took his supplies, and walked out leaving the clerk faintly scowling. The things he had toted up for the stranger weren't quite the staples most travelers bought. For instance, there was nothing that contained meat, there were chili peppers, cloves of garlic, flour, baking powder . . . and fifteen feet of thick hemp rope, too thick for roping, too long for a pigging string. If the stranger had a packhorse — hell — no one used a rope half as thick as a man's wrist for a lead shank.

The stranger returned to Jim Rourke's saloon for some watered whiskey and a smoke. The wind was rising again; dust appeared over the spindle doors, which made Jim growl. He told the stranger he'd thought several times about putting regular full-length doors in the place of those damned spindle doors. Every time the wind blew — and in springtime it nearly always did — roadway dust came into his saloon, which most folks could tolerate; it wasn't entirely the dust, it was also the odor that came with the dust. Calabasas was not a large settlement, but everyone either rode horses or drove them.

There were two old men dozing near a

dirty window, otherwise it was too early for the evening trade. Jim was a gregarious soul; right now all he had to converse with was the man who had visited his establishment twice today and seemed to be a nice-enough individual.

Jim rarely asked questions, particularly personal ones, and he rarely answered them. A man's business was his own; all Jim asked from mankind was that folks told the truth and did not steal. Beyond that, if they met the preacher's wife in the woodshed behind the parsonage, Jim would hold the door for them, or if a man needed to switch his young'un Jim would cut the stick for him.

But he skirted close to a personal question when he asked if the stranger figured to settle in town. The answer he got was accompanied with a smile. "No, but I've sure seen lots of places a man could settle in that aren't half as nice as this town."

Jim let the subject die. He would have refilled the customer's glass, but the man shook his head, put some coins atop the bar, nodded, and went back out into the now dying day. The town marshal was crossing from his jailhouse to the cafe, something the bronzed man watched for as long as Ed Ballinger was in sight.

Directly opposite the saloon was the wide

log gateway leading into the corralyard. Visible, despite the failing light, was a coach being readied for its run.

There was a lantern hanging from a tall pole. A lithe Mexican was climbing a ladder to light the lamp, which, even with the wick turned up, made very little impression on the descending night.

Down at the livery barn the old soldier, Enos Jordan, was putting ground barley from a bucket into the feed boxes of each stalled horse, using a dented coffee can. Every now and then he had to halt to wipe a running nose. When he turned and saw the man standing in the front opening to the runway, he had a two-second chill. The stranger was standing up there wide-legged and motionless, watching everything old Enos did.

The old man put down his bucket and can, shuffled ahead, and said, "You want your horse, mister?"

The other man sauntered into the runway. "That big bay over yonder."

Enos nodded. "The blacksmith said if you was of a mind you could leave your horse over there an' he'd work it in the morning."

The stranger said he might just do that and went to the harness room for his outfit. He did not ask the old soldier to lend a hand and kept back to the old man right up until he looped one rein around the horn. Holding the left rein in his hand, he said, "Stalled horses have troubles. They need exercise."

Enos nodded; what the man had said was the truth — but why not wait until daylight? Standing overnight wouldn't hurt the horse. Early morning was the ideal time to ride, if the damned wind wasn't blowing or it wasn't raining.

The stranger handed Enos a silver half-dollar, led his animal up front, and mounted just inside the runway where the wind didn't reach. By the time Enos raised his wet eyes from the unexpected but very welcome silver coin on his palm the stranger was no longer in sight.

Enos's throat burned, his stomach clutched and unclutched, water from his eyes trickled down his cheeks.

He knew better; he had been instructed very firmly by the liveryman never to leave the area at night, but right now, with money in his clenched fist, he *had* to leave.

He hurried up to the saloon, which had scant customers, leaned on the bar, and showed Jim his half-dollar.

Without a word Rourke went along the bar, reached below, and returned with a bottle. It contained the dregs from every glass Jim had served for almost two weeks. There was wine and whiskey, but mostly dead beer.

He took it down to the old soldier, placed it in front of him, and shook his head at the outstretched claw of a hand. "Keep it," he told the hostler. "You might want to buy something to eat."

Enos took his bottle to a dark corner, sat down and drank, paused to belch, drank some more, and this time raised a filthy cuff to push away the sweat blossoming over his face and neck.

His hand was as steady as stone when he opened it to admire the silver half dollar. Life was rotten, age was suffering, memories were torture, but every now and then someone came along to infuse something warm, something to erase the craving, to kindle afresh the feeling that all men were not sly, conniving sons of bitches.

Over at the bar Jim kept an eye on the old skeleton. When a fleshy-faced individual said, "It never stops amazing me how long they last. Jim . . . ?"

"Leave him be. What the hell, Doc. He's better off right now than he'd be if you took him in hand."

"He's killing himself."

Rourke's gaze came around. "He's already old, Doc. You may want to die in bed — me, I'd rather not live so long I can't even

wipe my own nose. Him . . . Doc, not everyone gets the chance to go out the way they
want to go . . . Care for a refill?"

"No thanks, one nightcap a day is my
quota. Good night, Jim."

"Good night, Doc."

3

While a Hard Wind Blew

Big Ed Ballinger enjoyed swapping lies with the loafers at Pete Bradley's poolroom two doors north of Rourke's saloon.

Ed was well liked throughout the community, even among the outlying cattle outfits. Being unattached, he was particularly welcome in most homes by womenfolk who felt no man should be single.

If there was any aversion to Ed, it was because like any lawman who remained in a community very long, he had, if not enemies, at least folks who did not like him very much.

Usually these were drunks he had collared, rambunctious rangemen who stormed into Calabasas to let off steam on Saturday nights. There was an occasional thief or fugitive, but as far as most folks knew, Ed was not the kind of man to make serious enemies. What

most folks did not know was that, entirely by accident, Ballinger had learned something about Henry Drake that would not have set well with the community, especially among womenfolk.

Ed was at the pool hall one midmorning when a stranger walked in, looking for a game. There were only three men in the place at the time: Ed, Pete Bradley, and the stranger.

Pete rarely played, especially for money. Ed was letting his breakfast settle. He nodded amiably at the stranger, who considered Ed's badge for a moment before asking if Ed would care to shoot a game with him.

Ed was good, but the stranger was very good. During the course of relieving the town marshal of two dollars, the stranger said he was from a farming community in Missouri. That he had been born and raised in that community, that he knew everyone for miles around, which was customary, and he also said he remembered folks pretty well.

There was a pause while Marshal Ballinger handed over the four bits he had just lost, the balls were racked up, and the next game started. This time the stranger, a man of middle years, was quiet for quite a spell as though concentrating on the game, then, as Ed leaned to play, the stranger asked a question.

"That feller who runs the general store — you known him long?"

Ed nodded and watched his ball miss and sink into a pocket. He sighed over his misfortune and answered almost without thinking. "Henry Drake? I've known him since I come here, and to hear it told, he come here about the time the army pulled out an' Calabasas began to grow."

The stranger leaned with his cue, his shrewd gaze on the scattered balls. "That might be about right. I was a kid when a feller name of Henry Drake left his wife and three chil'run an' run off with a redheaded widow named Bertha Batson. Years later it was rumored around our town that Bertha died of a busted neck when a buggy horse run away with her and rolled 'em both down a couple hunnert feet of rocks."

The stranger straightened up, having barely missed sinking his ball. As Ed Ballinger stepped up and crouched, the stranger said, "Old Doc Pemberton buried folks in our town. The story we commenced hearin' right after Bertha was buried was that her neck was broke before the accident. She was already dead when somethin' spooked that buggy horse over the cliff. Doc said there wasn't no blood, that folks already dead don't bleed."

Ed shot, missed, slowly straightened around to look steadily at the stranger. "What town was that?" he asked.

"Rileyville." This time the stranger did not move to the table. He and Ed Ballinger stood gazing at each other until Ed said, "Drake's a common name, friend. So is Henry."

The stranger nodded. "Yes, sir, but not too many folks got a little scar on the chin an' a sort of bent first joint of their forefinger on the right hand, do they?"

Ed said no more. He and the stranger played two more games, then the stranger had to quit because the afternoon southbound stage would be leaving directly. Before departing, he said he was on his way out to California to visit his sister.

After he was gone, Ed swore at himself; he had forgotten to ask the traveler his name. He racked his cue, strolled over where Pete Bradley was reading an old newspaper, and asked if by any chance Pete had heard the stranger's name. Pete shook his head. He was not only hard of hearing but had been concentrating on reading his newspaper; Pete only just barely knew how to read.

Ed had an early supper and was leaning out front, having a smoke, when Henry Drake came up from the store. When they met, Ed Ballinger asked if Henry had a moment, then asked him if he'd ever heard of a town called Rileyville in Missouri.

Ed was an observant man; most longtime lawmen were. He saw the shock arrive and swiftly depart as Henry shook his head. "Nope, never did. Why?"

"I met a feller at the poolroom a while back. He was real good, cleaned me out for two dollars. He was from that town."

"What was his name?"

"Well, y'know I should have asked and plumb forgot to. He was goin' out to California, that's about all I know. . . . Henry, he was born an' raised in Rileyville."

Ballinger watched the merchant closely. Henry had recovered from shock, but now he had narrowed eyes as he said, "I came from Missouri, Ed, but I never heard of a place called Rileyville."

"Henry, the barber missed shavin' that little scar on your chin."

Drake raised his right hand to his face. Ballinger said, "I never noticed you had a busted finger before."

Drake lowered his hand to wiggle the lumpy forefinger. "No. Doc says it's the rheumatics. It settles in different places. I'm lucky, he said, it didn't settle in my knee or neck, places that really cripple folks. Ed . . . about this feller from Missouri . . ."

Big Ed Ballinger smiled broadly. "Just makin' talk, Henry. Go ahead an' eat or the counter'll be crowded."

Drake stood a moment, watching the large man strolling in the direction of his jailhouse. Drake had known the town marshal a long time, and one thing had impressed him: Ballinger's easygoing, affable attitude masked a shrewd, knowledgeable power of observation.

He entered the cafe with much less appetite than he'd left the store with.

He did not finish his meal but he had three cups of black java and by the time he had drained the last one he made up his mind. Maybe Ed was as he'd said, just making talk, but if that was so, why had he mentioned Rileyville out of hundreds of towns in Missouri? The past could ruin him; he could not take the chance.

The wind was skirling again, the night was dark and stormy with spitting rain squalls. Henry rode out of town the following morning, bundled to the gullet, picked his way eastward to that old Anasazi pueblo, made his compact out there, and returned to Calabasas after nightfall. If anyone had noticed his departure or return nothing was said.

The following day he saw Halcón in town. The day after his meeting with Ballinger in front of the cafe there was no sign of Halcón. Henry opened the store, told his clerk he was going to the cafe, which he did, but afterward he also went up to the saloon.

Jim Rourke nodded woodenly. He could not recall ever having served liquor to Henry Drake before evening, but then, as he told himself, his memory wasn't all it had once been. Besides, he did not care for Henry Drake; if he had served him other mornings years past he would have performed it as a perfunctory duty with no conversation involved and no reason to recall it.

There was a distraction. A stage driver named Bellamy called over for some liquid fortification after bucking bad weather all the way north from a town called Spencerville. As Rourke set up his jolt, the whip, a ruddy, sinewy man, looked across at the barman and said, "Damnedest thing, Jim. Maybe two miles south of town where there's a pine tree about a hunnert feet from the road, there was a hangrope."

Rourke and Henry Drake faced the whip. Rourke said, "Hangrope?"

The whip nodded, dropped his jolt straight down, and blew out a long, ragged breath before speaking again. "Yeah, a hangrope with a hangman's knot. Looked to me to have been tied by someone who knew how them

40

things is made. It was just hangin' there in plain sight of the road. I had three passengers, travelin' men from the looks of them, they was sound asleep . . . I didn't slack off."

"Anyone down there?" Rourke asked.

"Well, it was close to sunrise, so I wasn't sure, but I think there was a feller sittin' a horse on a little hill off easterly a ways, but the light was real poor an' he was some distance off. An' I had my rig and hitch to mind. I wouldn't swear I even seen him, but if I didn't, it sure as hell looked like someone settin' out there with a measly sky behind him."

"Did you tell Ed?" Rourke asked.

The whip nodded and pushed his little sticky glass forward for a refill. He had been battered by wind, cold, and lashing rain. He was tired to the bone, a condition he had experienced often during his years of tooling stagecoaches, but he knew the antidote — two jolts of popskull.

As he reached for the refill he nodded at Rourke. "I run Ed down. He was killin' time in the harness shop. I told him. He said if there was fixin' to be a hangin' he wanted to know. He hiked toward his jailhouse faster'n I've ever seen him move."

Henry Drake returned to his store. He absentmindedly took care of several customers, then told the clerk to mind customers while he sorted and pigeonholed the mail, which he did almost without thinking; he had owned the Calabasas mail franchise for years. He needed only to glance at a name to know which little box to stuff mail into.

He was worried. He had not seen Marshal Ballinger ride south out of town, but he knew Ed had done that because several diners at the cafe had commented on it, curious as folks always were when the marshal left town.

Henry had a poor appetite, but he drank coffee before returning to the store.

Those black clouds were up there again, roiling and spitting occasional lashings of rain, but most tiresome of all, the wind scoured roadways down to hardpan, intruded into the saloon, blew fine dust into the general store, made drifts of the stuff against buildings, and drove most folks indoors, where they waited it out with closed windows and edgy nerves. There was nothing that could fray nerves and shorten tempers like the wind.

Animals disliked it as much as people: they would turn tail and drift ahead of it exactly as they did during winter blizzards.

Travelers, exposed to its capricious, sudden changes of direction, wore themselves out bracing into it.

Ed Ballinger's big horse slogged down the road with its eyes pinched nearly closed and blew its nose often. Ed sat atop warm inside his riding coat, a bandana tied across his lower face, watching the road from beneath a tipped-down hatbrim.

He almost did not see the pine tree; might not have if that hangrope hadn't been jerking and twisting as the wind tore the tree.

He halted on the roadbed and sat hunched, peering. Well, at least there wasn't someone hanging there, which was what had troubled him on the long ride. He wagged his head; what sense did it make to leave a hangrope draped from a tree within sight of the road? Why wasn't there someone dangling from the rope with a broken neck?

He reined off the road toward the tree and squinted roundabout but with particular attention at a low hill without a shred of brush or grass. That's where Bellamy had said he'd seen the horseman.

Well, if there'd been a horseman, something the whip had not seemed certain of, he sure as hell wasn't over there now. Maybe poor visibility, shadows, or something had made it seem there had been a rider sitting up there, watching the road.

Ed thought he would ride atop the knoll after he took down the hangrope; if there were tracks up there and, an even bigger *if,* the wind hadn't scoured them out of existence . . .

Ed drew rein, sat briefly watching the wildly swinging rope, and noticed it was new rope and that, as Bellamy had noted, whoever had wrapped the knot knew what he was doing. He swung to the ground to lead his horse closer.

The rope had been tied to a stout limb slightly higher than a man on horseback could reach, even standing in his stirrups.

If a man stood on his saddle . . . the only damned idiots Ed had ever seen do that was a touring band of Mexican *charros* who had passed through. During their performance at Calabasas, several of them had stood on their saddles, jumping through ropes.

Ballinger was a stockman, who used horses and equipment for work, not games. He wondered about climbing the damned tree, which had as many intervening limbs as a porcupine had quills. To cut that hangrope, Ballinger would have to shed his coat, the sweater under it, and do something he hadn't even been good at as a child: climb a knotty old pine tree.

He led his horse to a nearby big bush, made him fast, and returned to the hangrope, and looked up. He thought of trying to shoot the rope apart. Ballinger was better than average with a handgun, but doubted he'd be able to tear the rope, even if he shot his weapon empty.

He cursed the man who had tied that rope up there. He squinted in all directions, saw nothing, and looked at the ground. Again, nothing. If the rope had been put up there last night, between squall rain and hard wind, there would not now be tracks to see.

Nor were there.

He resented what he thought was a prank. Or maybe a sign to frighten someone. Whatever the reason for the rope, one thing was certain: it had not been draped from the tree for a lynching. If that had been the case there would be a corpse twisting and swaying in the wind.

Ballinger pulled his hat hard down, shoved his riding gloves into his pockets, and stepped directly to the spot where the swinging rope had to come past. He missed it the first time and got himself set to try again, standing at his full height with both arms overhead.

He did not hear a thing. The wind was gusting when Ballinger stretched upright to grab the rope, fully exposed, and the bullet struck.

He did not even gasp; he simply dropped, dead before he hit the ground.

His tethered horse had heard something and was peering intently in the direction of the little hill, but gave that up when there was no second gunshot, no scent, and no movement.

4

Aftermath

Walt Bellamy was tooling the southbound coach the following morning on a magnificently clear, balmy day, the kind that commonly marked the departure of spring and the advent of summer. He had neglected to shave at the corralyard bunkhouse because the night before he had taken on enough of a load to insure he would sleep like the dead, which is exactly what he had done.

A Mexican yardman worriedly tugged on his arm to waken him. The yardman gestured to the coach, which was being hitched. Two passengers were already aboard and some light freight was being loaded into the boot.

Bellamy scrambled. He did not have to bother with a belt because he wore braces, and he reached the high seat to take the lines as the company manager appeared in the office doorway. Bellamy nodded, kicked the binders off, rattled the lines, and made the wide sashay past the gates into the roadway.

47

He walked the outfit a full mile before whistling the horses into an easy lope. He hadn't eaten since the night before, his eyes felt wet, his face bristled with salt-and-pepper stubble, and his mouth tasted like the bottom of a bird cage.

He hadn't looked inside at his passengers. He drove almost without conscious effort; he knew the route and the road as well as he knew the back of his hand, so he had time to consider several things, one of which was the effects on a man who drank on an empty stomach then went to bed, another was the everlasting sameness of his job and the notion that a man who spent his mature years looking at the butts of horses had to eventually recognize that unless he lifted his eyes a little higher, he was going to die with a very limited outlook.

But at least it was a beautiful day. After weeks of rain, thunder, darkness at midday, lightning, washed-out roadbeds, and that infernal wind, Walt Bellamy only had to stop thinking of himself and raise his eyes to feel the exaltation that imbued outdoorsmen when a beautiful, genuine springtime day arrived. A couple of miles south of town, he was breathing deeply, admiring the soft-scented springtime warmth, the stillness, when he saw the same hangrope he had seen before, still dangling, and nearby a large saddle horse tethered and impatiently pawing.

Bellamy did not notice the dead man until one of the passengers called out and pointed with a rigid arm.

He eased back on the lines, gently applied the binders until the coach stopped. Then he sat like a knot on a log, staring.

The passenger who had yelled climbed out and walked briskly toward the lone pine tree. He was a rangeman, spare, faded-looking, nondescript, until he slowly turned and Walt could see his face, which he would not forget as long as he lived. The rangeman yelled, "He's got a badge on his shirt, an' he was shot through the brisket."

Another passenger alighted. Only the third passenger, a woman in her middle years, remained inside. Even Bellamy climbed down and set the binders hard, before walking in the direction of the tree.

When he halted, he did not say a word. Neither did the other two men until the rawboned rangeman sighed and said, "Driver, ain't that your lawman from back yonder? I seen him at the mercantile day afore yestiddy."

Bellamy nodded woodenly, then slowly raised his eyes and looked roundabout. His gaze touched, and passed, that little easterly knoll. Recovering from the shock, he said, "Lend me a hand. We'll put him in the boot."

As the second passenger stepped up to help, he said, "Driver, I got to be down at Haggardtown before nightfall."

Bellamy's retort was short. "Mister, it'll only take an hour to go back two miles, leave Ed, then strike out again. You'll be down there by nightfall."

The reassured passenger, a traveling man, was placated. The three of them carried the corpse, jackknifed it into the boot — which wasn't easy, Ballinger was not very limber — and as Walt Bellamy passed the stage door he looked in, expecting the woman to look horrified, but she looked back at him from gray eyes with her mouth as tight as a trap. Evidently she was not a greenhorn.

Bellamy got the hitch reversed and made good time returning. Folks who saw him coming back watched until he pulled into the corralyard, where the company manager came out wearing a black scowl. Bellamy called a yard man, and together they carried the corpse out of the way. Bellamy nodded to the head In'ian and without a word went up the side of his coach, sashayed around the yard, cleared both gates, turned southward without looking right or left, and yelled his hitch into a lope.

He had known Ed Ballinger six years, had liked him, and right now felt no hunger, no furry tongue, no resentfulness about his job, and did not even admire the beautiful day.

Ballinger's six-gun still had the tie-down thong holding it in its holster. Most likely he hadn't had any warning. A shot like that, right through the heart, didn't even allow for the two or three seconds required to draw a breath.

Doc Williams, who was old, drank too much and, being a bachelor, shaved every other day, always had cigar ash on his front, and wore glasses as thick as the bottom of a whiskey bottle. He examined the corpse in his little embalming shed off the kitchen, where the smell of embalming fluid mingled with cooking scents, and told Martin Bedford, the disagreeable, surly, hard-driving corral-yard boss, that Ballinger had died instantly, and from what Doc had heard, the marshal had walked right into a classical example of a bushwhack.

Martin, who had not liked Ed Ballinger very much, sipped whiskey at the kitchen table with Doctor Williams and said disagreeably, "Well, no one forced him to wear that badge, did they?"

Doc's faded pale eyes fixed on the younger

man. "The devil himself don't deserve to die like that."

Martin Bedford left. Doc's visitors continued to drop by to view the corpse, listen to Doc's pronouncements, and have a drink with him, until long after nightfall, by which time Doc left the naked corpse on the table and couldn't find his behind using both hands.

Walt Bellamy arrived back in town the following afternoon, still unshaven but clear-eyed and as solemn as an owl. He told and retold his story so many times he wearied of hearing himself and retired to the bunk-house where he took an all-over bath in a trough, shaved, put on clean clothes, and went out into the alley where he would be unseen. He smoked two cigarettes while squatting in the shadows, staring at nothing. It wasn't just the death of a friend that troubled him, it was the way Ed Ballinger had died. Murder pure and simple. He did not consider who had killed his friend nor why. Not right then, anyway. He mourned the loss in his own way: alone.

At the mercantile Henry Drake's shock was genuine for about an hour. He then joined the community in lamenting Ballinger's death, and was as fervent in his denunciation of whoever had performed the bushwhack as anyone in town.

He even went up to the saloon after hours and joined in the profane, loud, and fierce pronouncements of grisly retribution if the bushwhacker was found, which, as the night wore on and Jim Rourke's nectar flowed, became louder, less comprehensible, and more ludicrous.

They buried Marshal Ballinger two days later. The entire town turned out, even those who had genuinely disliked Ed, or like the corralyard boss Martin Bedford, had not so much disliked Ballinger as they didn't like authority of any kind.

Among the mourners were a great number of people from Mex-town. Ed had been respected in Mex-town for his evenhanded justice, his good nature, and his willingness to take complaints seriously.

He had neither disparaged nor ignored the people of Mex-town. For his time, Ed Ballinger was unique and was respected.

Among the mourners in ragged pants, clutching old sombreros to their chests as the minister spoke, was Arturo Valdez. He was older than dirt, with close-spaced, sunk-set tawny-tan dark eyes and a mouth that puckered as it fell inward. He should have been one of the elders of Mex-town except that he was not a native, and had in fact only appeared down there a few weeks before — from

53

where, no one asked and old Arturo did not say. It was enough that he was one of them, very poor, very old, a *peon*, ignored by the inhabitants of Gringo-town, an old fagot hunter with his ancient burro who lived in an abandoned *jacal* that was dilapidated and unclean even by Mex-town standards.

When the minister spoke his prayer, old Arturo Valdez moved his lips in Spanish and smiled. In Mex-town he was known as *Des Molacho* because he had no teeth.

Jim Rourke watched the old Mexican and muttered to the man beside him in the throng. "Ed was fair with Mexicans, which is more'n can be said of most folks. Look at that old screwt, smilin' an' prayin' like he knows what he's doing."

The other man, lean, slightly hawk-faced, showed even white teeth as he softly replied, "Maybe he does."

Rourke turned with widening eyes. "Hell, I haven't seen you round town the last week or so. I figured you'd rode on."

"I went among the cow outfits, lookin' for work."

"No luck?"

"No."

Rourke returned his attention to the minister and the squared-up hole at his feet. "Folks'll miss Ed. I sure will. I'd give new

54

money to know who bushwhacked him."

The lean stranger also watched as the body was lowered. He filed past with the others to drop a handful of moist soil into the grave. Once, his raised eyes met those of the old *peon* with no teeth, then he passed along, heading for his horse as the crowd began to break up. There were buggies, wagons, even some donkey carts.

Only the people from Mex-town appeared to have come on foot. It wasn't much of a hike; the cemetery was roughly a half mile northeast of town among some trees the founders of modern Calabasas had planted years earlier. And it was another magnificent day with clear visibility to the farthest curve of the world, an unblemished turquoise sky, a warming earth putting forth grass and tiny lavender flowers called *alfilaria* by the bushel.

Winter's last fierce struggle to linger seemed to have been overcome by summer's advent.

But someone like Martin Bedford, in whom bedrock cynicism was thoroughly embedded, allowed no one he met to believe for one moment lasting good weather had arrived.

He told Henry Drake over the counter at the general store that he'd seen a number of springtimes that had lasted almost to autumn with storms, floods, collapsed buildings as sodden earth gave way beneath them, and dozens of drowned people.

Henry had not argued. He was no more fond of Martin Bedford than most folks were. The difference was that since Martin ran a monthly account at the store, he had tolerated him, but now with the account two months past due, regardless of what Martin might say, the past due account was uppermost in Henry's mind.

He mentioned it. "It costs a lot of money to keep my shelves stocked, Martin. The mercantile business is like any other business — I got to lay out a lot of cash to have what folks want, an' the only way I can keep the store stocked is if —"

"Henry, business has been bad since last summer. I'm cuttin' corners every way I can. I'm down to two yardmen an' doin' my own repairs."

Henry listened expressionlessly. "Martin, I got to do somethin' I never done before. I got to start layin' on a six-percent charge for overdue accounts."

For a moment the dark, surly man seemed ready to explode, and Henry spoke quickly in a placating tone of voice. "Let's say folks don't pay you for haulin' their freight. You got men to pay, animals to feed, harness an' such like to keep up —"

"That's exactly what part of my trouble is," Bedford exclaimed. "I got bills for haulin' freight, back almost a year. I rode myself ragged tryin' to collect, an' meantime I got feed to pay for, shoein', wages . . ." Bedford's face hardened. "Six percent? You can't do that. I'll pay up as soon as business picks up."

"Martin, I got to charge six percent. It's the only way I can recover from puttin' out so much of my own money to keep the store stocked."

"I'll see you in hell," Bedford exclaimed and stamped out of the store.

Henry looked over to his clerk, who had been listening, and rolled his eyes. The younger man went back to work with a feather duster. When he had first come to Calabasas he had worked as a yardman for Martin Bedford. For six months, until the opening had appeared at the mercantile, he had suffered abuse, routine cussing-out, even a time or two something close to physical blows.

As he now dusted shelves he wondered if his present employer hadn't made a mistake. He disliked Martin Bedford with a full heart, but he was by nature too philosophical, too fatalistic, or maybe just too unsure of himself to think in terms of revenge.

As for his present employer, there were

things he disapproved of. Henry Drake thought only of money. He had refused credit to hungry squatters, had cheated them on their eggs and smoked hams, had lied with a straight face when they had almost begged for a better offer on the produce they raised on starved-out homesteads. He even added hidden charges to the monthly accounts of cowmen, and although to the clerk's knowledge no one had called him yet on that, he had served those cowmen ever since he'd come to work at the mercantile. There wasn't one of them who would not yank the slack out of Mister Drake if he found out, and inevitably someday one of them would find out.

Mister Drake left early, which left it up to the clerk to close up after the last customer departed just shy of five o'clock.

As the clerk turned from locking the door he noticed the lean rangeman with the hawklike features meeting a very old toothless Mexican in front of the harness shop. They nodded and spoke very briefly; the *viejo* held out his hand, which the stranger seemed to barely touch with his palm before drawing his hand back in a loose fist as he nodded and the old Mexican shuffled off.

It was nothing. Two dark-skinned men, one young, one old, greeting each other fleetingly.

Amos Lawton rattled the door to be sure it was locked and headed for the cafe. He had no family; lived at the roominghouse where other single men lived.

He might have paused at Rourke's saloon, but he would not be paid for another three days.

The beautiful day passed over into a beautiful evening with faint stars in a flawless high canopy.

At Jim Rourke's place there was some desultory discussion about a successor to Ed Ballinger. Possibilities were mentioned: one was the hulking man who worked for the blacksmith, but those who knew the helper wagged their heads. If all he had to do was yank out the slack he would do fine, but no one had ever seen him wearing a sidearm. Others demurred on the grounds that while he was big and stout enough, he was too slow in the head to last long.

Another name or two was proposed. There was dissension again, and finally the project was abandoned in favor of alleviating a lot of scorched throats. Besides, Ed had only been in his grave a few days, nothing untoward had occurred in that time, and as some men had said, Calabasas was generally an orderly place, except maybe on some Saturday nights, so there was no big hurry to find a new town marshal.

There was more to it than that, however: Ed Ballinger had been a friend to every man in the saloon, and they were uncomfortable with that discussion. It seemed almost as though they had not sorrowed enough over his killing.

Three days after the funeral Henry Drake was standing in front of his store, flour-sack apron in place, when his heart skipped two beats; Mister Halcón had ridden past in the middle of the roadway. He had glanced in Henry's direction, acted as though he had not seen the merchant, and kept on riding.

Henry put in a bad night. He thought of several unpleasant reasons why Halcón would still be in the countryside. One was blackmail; that thought curdled his blood. Another possibility, which he liked even less, was that Halcón might need another three hundred dollars and Henry had no one he had to fear after Ballinger. How could he say no to a killer?

The final reason made him throw back the blankets, perch on the edge of the bed, and grope in darkness for his bottle of whiskey.

Halcón should have been long gone. Henry's understanding of killers was limited, but common sense told him a man of Halcón's profession would not ordinarily remain in an area where he had committed murder. Ordinarily.

5

The Highwayman

This time the lean, coppery-skinned man did not have to seek shelter from bad weather at Anasazi Pueblo, and the feed was better for his big thoroughbred-looking horse.

The horse cropped grass as his rider hunkered in pleasant sunlight to smoke and occasionally view the trails down from the mesa.

He had been there an hour. There was no hurry; he had the patience of someone who had all eternity to sit and wait.

As before, the big bay horse raised its head, stopped chewing, and stared at a downward path until a rider appeared, this time riding a better animal and sitting his saddle like someone who had done his share of saddlebacking.

The bronzed man stubbed out his smoke, arose, and waited. He was seen the moment he stood up; in a huge, empty land where silence and stillness prevailed, movement was critical.

The rider came down to the old pueblo on a loose rein. He too was dark, with no spare meat. He appeared to be about Halcón's age, but something like that was almost indefinable. He was unlike the other man Halcón had met out here: This rider dismounted, called out a greeting, and walked forward without once taking his eyes off the hawk-faced man. He even smiled, not a pleasant expression but one that clearly indicated he met Halcón as an equal.

Halcón smiled back genially as he said, "Beautiful weather for a change."

Martin Bedford agreed. "Very nice. The air smells good, roadbeds are hard for heavy rigs . . . How much?"

"Three hundred dollars. Who?"

"I think I've seen you in town. Do you know the bastard who runs the general store?"

Halcón nodded. "Henry Drake?"

"That's him."

Halcón held out a hand, and neither man looked away from the other as the money changed hands. As Halcón was pocketing it, he said, "These things take time."

"As much as you need. Just do it." The surly man cocked his head slightly. "Did you know a man named Ed Ballinger?"

Halcón was already approaching his horse.

With his back to Bedford, he removed the hobbles, tightened the cinch, swung across leather, and still with his back to the other man, started up one of the ancient paths to the mesa.

Martin Bedford watched the tall horse go up the path in powerful strides, and said, "I'll be damned. . . . *Sure as hell, he's the one who did it!*"

The perfect weather made folks believe the blustery, fierce springtime was past. Womenfolk were out turning warm earth for vegetable gardens, dragooning their young'uns to help. It was sweaty work but it was vital.

Men were expanding their horizons too. Several had scoured the country where Ed Ballinger had died, but even if they hadn't waited for good weather to go down there, they would have found nothing; there had been too much rain and wind.

They examined Ballinger's horse and saddle. Alex Jobey, the slovenly liveryman with the close-set eyes, told them they were wasting their time. He had already gone over the marshal's outfit, had found no dark stains, no signs of anything except everyday use. He summed up his conclusions cryptically.

"Ed was shot where they found him. He wasn't nowhere near his horse. Doc told me the slug blew his heart apart, that Ed was dead before he hit the ground. Did you gents find anythin' down yonder?"

They hadn't.

The beautiful weather continued. This time of year when winter's pent-up energies drove people to fresh undertakings made it impossible for the mystery surrounding Ballinger's murder to be kept alive; they would never forget him, but the shock passed. Ed Ballinger became the subject of infrequent speculation. In time, all the theories would be mentioned. Also in time, the marshal would fade as a topic of interest. Life went on. This was helped by a sudden unseasonable return of bad weather, a killing frost that destroyed all the budding life in everyone's vegetable patch. That took precedence over just about everything else, because the only greens folks lived on during harsh winters came from rows of bottled produce.

The vegetables had to be replanted, which was not altogether unusual — killing late frosts had come before, but this one encouraged cynics like Martin Bedford to say, "I told you so."

Another incident riveted local interest, something that had not happened in the Calabasas area in at least five years.

One of the local stages was stopped five miles north of town and robbed of four mail sacks, a small steel-bound box of money destined for the Calabasas general store, and every item of jewelry and cash from four passengers.

Martin Bedford went before the town council in a fiercely denunciatory mood. He was not the only one: the husbands of two of the passengers were local cattlemen who had riders scouring the area where the holdup had occurred while the ranchers themselves appeared before the same town council and made threats. These were taken more seriously by the councilmen than the anger of the stage company's man.

Henry Drake was also present at the council meeting. He made the only reasonable complaint. "If you had replaced Ed Ballinger . . . but no, you sat on your butts. Now we don't have no lawman. What're you goin' to do, wait until the word spreads far'n wide that Calabasas's got no lawman so's outlaws can come from all directions? I lost six hunnert dollars in cash in that robbery. I'm goin' to hold you gents accountable."

One councilman — Jim Rourke — said the same thing to every complainant: "Even if Ed had been alive, or if we'd found a feller to take his place . . . highwaymen strike without no warning. The damned robbery would still have happened. We could've had a whole regiment of U.S. Marshals in town — until the stage got to town no one would have known what happened."

Henry stood up and pointed a finger at Rourke. "Jim, if we'd just had a lawman, if folks had known we had one again, it might not have happened. I'll tell you somethin' else. If you don't replace Ed, if you don't get a tough, hard-ridin' lawman, it'll happen again."

The entire town was incensed, although only Henry Drake had suffered any substantial loss. Mostly, the stage passengers were passing through. They remained overnight and added their indignation to all the other denunciatory comments.

The rangemen who went out to search found nothing except some shod-horse tracks that had come from the north to the ambushing site, and had afterward gone back in the same direction. From this the obvious conclusion was drawn: the highwayman was not a local man. That Drake's money box had been aboard was thought to be pure coincidence; the highwayman had been just plain lucky.

It had happened before; almost everyone knew a story of at least one such lucky raid by highwaymen. And truth be told, folks were not sorry Henry had lost his money box.

Later, they would even laugh about it.

But Henry reacted as though he had been injured to the heart. He didn't let a day pass where he didn't complain bitterly to his customers. His clerk had to listen to all sorts of accusations of incompetence by the town council, even some dark insinuations that one of those miserable sons of bitches might have been the actual highwayman.

As days passed and good weather returned, people returned to their normal pursuits, by which time it was becoming amusing to hear Henry rant.

Then abruptly Henry stopped ranting, became secretive, and assumed an attitude of unnatural geniality, which appeared to his clerk, who knew Drake inside and out, as an almost disgusting variety of hypocrisy, even as the clerk wondered about the change.

If others noticed, they probably decided Henry had become reconciled to his loss and was adjusting to it, even though geniality was not known to be part of his character.

This too diminished in importance as time passed. Cowmen appeared in town, still growling about the highwayman their riders had been unable to track beyond a glass-rock area about nine miles north.

But springtime was marking time. Their indignation faded as work piled up, until about two weeks after the robbery, at the height of the springtime working season, they neither appeared in town nor more than occasionally recalled the robbery.

It was shortly before life had returned to normal that Henry sold some horse salve and some clear windowpane rawhide to an old Mexican whose toothless smile and ragged appearance made Henry ask to see money before going after the purchases.

That was when the old man smiled. He placed two gold coins atop the counter. As Henry went to fetch the purchases, the wrinkled old *peon* watched him from weasel-sharp brown eyes.

The old Mexican had dropped a scrap of paper as he withdrew his hand from a trouser pocket to show Henry the gold coins. After the old man shuffled away with his purchases, Henry noticed the crumpled paper and went to pick it up with the intention of tossing it into a trash barrel. As he approached the barrel he unfolded the paper, and while his Spanish was not the best, he had lived among Mexicans enough years to have picked up enough to carry on a simple conversation.

He took the paper behind the counter, spread it flat, leaned over, and studied it. Some of the words had been scrawled by a shaky hand in misspelled and difficult Spanish, but the drawing was readable. A word that stumped Henry was *sepultar* but he had no trouble with the word *dinero* nor the word *caja;* some of his stock for the store came from places where Spanish was the only word used to denote a box.

The scrap of paper was small and rumpled, but its map was clear enough despite the wrinkles and ragged edges. The paper was old and limp.

He took it to his dingy office, closed the door, and laboriously interpreted the map. It began with a cross above something that resembled a square with a domed roof.

His heart was pounding. The only structure with a cross where roadways led toward a plaza was the ancient Spanish mission in Mextown. He pushed sweat off his forehead with a sleeve, opened a desk drawer, lifted out the bottle, took a couple of swallows, and leaned over the scrap of paper again.

He worked out the routes shown on the little map in his mind, settled on the exact mark where it said *sepultar*, and leaned back; he had to find someone who could interpret *sepultar* into English, otherwise it was clear to Henry that a *caja* with *dinero* was buried there.

He told his clerk he would be gone for a while and went up to Jim Rourke's saloon.

Rourke spoke Spanish like a native.

But Henry had no intention of being direct. He leaned on the bar, smiled genially, and asked for a glass of beer. He started a conversation with Rourke by mentioning the way business seemed to pick up with good weather and asked if the saloon trade was increasing. Most merchants, in fact most human beings, could be drawn out when a subject was brought up that impinged on their personal well-being.

Jim unbent a little. Business, he said, had increased lately, what with travelers passing through and freighters using the roads again. He asked how the store was doing. Henry spread both hands atop the bar. "I think business is getting better." He thought of something and also said, "But I got accounts in arrears that're makin' it hard."

Rourke, who neither liked Henry Drake nor sympathized with him, shrugged. "You're in the wrong business. In a saloon, you get paid when you set 'em up."

Henry nodded. "But I got to pay my suppliers. For instance I got some leather goods out of Messico a few days back, an' they'll expect their money. I got to strain a little, but I'll make it. By the way, one of them Mex crates has the word *sepultar* painted on it. That's not the name of the outfit I

71

bought the goods from."

Jim gazed steadily at Henry Drake for a moment before speaking. "You know what *sepultar* means?" Before Drake could answer, Rourke leaned on the counter and stared at Henry. "Let me ask you a personal question, Henry. Are you runnin' guns?"

Drake looked shocked. "What kind of a question is that? I'm not runnin' guns an' never have."

"Well, Henry, *sepultar* means a secret place. On a box it might mean there was something hid inside, maybe not guns, Mexicans buy guns *from* us, they wouldn't be sneakin' guns up here. Maybe it means there's something inside the box like some kind of contraband from down there."

Henry drained his glass and felt sweat on his face. His hands were unsteady so he pocketed them. Rourke was staring at him. "There was leather goods in the damned box, Jim — braided Mex reins an' headstalls, some of them monkey-face *tapaderas* Mexicans use. Nothing else."

"Did you look real good, Henry? I don't understand why some Mex would put that word on your box of leather goods."

Henry smiled weakly. "A joke?"

Rourke frowned. "Why? That's no joke. If the army had come onto that box they'd have busted it open, an' your butt would have been in a sling. Secret hiding places aren't funny to the army."

Henry's dilemma had him sweating like a stud horse. He'd had no idea that damned word and his simple inquiry concerning it would cause this situation. He asked Rourke for a refill, and when the saloonman went to get it Henry did some fast thinking. When Jim returned he drained half the glass and said Rourke made some of the best brew he'd ever tasted.

Jim studied the merchant. The affability hadn't really bothered him, but a compliment from Henry Drake did. Henry paid and walked out of the saloon with fresh sweat bursting out all over. Even the pleasant dryness of a lovely day did not stop the sweating.

He returned to the store, ignoring the surprised look of his clerk, and went into the dingy office, closed the door, and sat down. He had it figured out, but while doing so he had sure as hell put a bee in Jim Rourke's bonnet, which was exactly what he had wanted to avoid.

He bent over the little scrap of paper again, sweat dripping from his chin, and went over the route of the map with a finger. He did this twice before easing back in the chair to consider loose ends. For one thing, where did that old Mexican get that piece of paper? For another thing, since he surely had known what was on it, would he have already dug up the box with money in it — which as sure as gawd made green apples was the money in Henry's little steel-bound box the highwayman had taken?

Finally, if the highwayman had hidden his loot in Mex-town, sure as hell he was a Mexican. Henry left the office in a hurry. He reached the corralyard as the late-day stage was departing.

Martin Bedford was inside the palisaded gate, watching Walt Bellamy navigate the gates without bumping a hub. He saw Henry, but ignored him until the coach was out of sight. Then he turned and snarled, "Six percent! You goddamn thief, Henry. I told you — I'll see you in hell before I'll let you rob me like that."

As Bedford turned abruptly toward his office, Henry reached swiftly to grab him by the arm. His face was red, his eyes constantly moving. "I didn't come over here about the account."

"Take your hand off my arm!"

Henry recoiled from the deadly glare of the surly man. "Listen! Was that highwayman a Messican?"

Bedford considered Henry's evident agita-

tion before answering. "His face was covered
. . . The driver said he was wearing Chihuahua
spurs, so I'd say he was a Mexican. I've never
seen regular rangemen wear them things."

Henry said, "Thanks," and left the yard,
moving fast. Martin Bedford gazed after him
with cold disdain, muttering that Drake was
getting as crazy as a 'coon, went into his
office, slammed the door, and shook his head.
Crazy or not, Henry wouldn't be around to
overcharge folks much longer.

Bedford crossed to the saloon, growled for
whiskey, and took both the bottle and the
glass to a distant table. Jim Rourke decided
the stage company's man had something on
his mind.

From half the length of the empty room
Bedford called to sarcastically ask if the town
council had found a replacement yet for Ed
Ballinger.

Jim reddened and made a savage swipe of
the bartop with his old rag as he called back,
"No!"

"What are you waiting for — the Second
Coming? I got stages running every blessed
day. Jim, if the council don't do something
soon, I'll find someone an' if necessary I'll
pay him out'n my own pocket!"

Rourke leaned on his counter, clenching
the damp rag for several seconds, before turn-

ing his back on Bedford and walking over to a tub of greasy water with glasses in it, which he proceeded to remove one by one and dry with fierce gestures.

6

A Long Night

Henry had an early supper, then went home to look for the six-gun. He shoved it into his front waistband, put on a dark coat, and went out back to a shed for a shovel.

Dusk had come and gone: it was a beautiful, balmy night with a high rash of stars and a scimitar moon.

He would have enjoyed a stogie, but cigars required time and Henry was in a hurry to dig up his stolen six hundred dollars — if that damned malevolent-eyed Mexican hadn't already dug it up.

The old man had paid for purchases with gold coins. Henry's money in the box would be greenback paper notes with a piece of string around each hundred dollars, the way the Denver bank had been sending him money for years. So that old wrinkled, toothless, ragged *peon* had got his gold money somewhere else. Right now what concerned Henry Drake was that as prominent as he was in the Calabasas community, if he appeared down in Mex-town carrying a shovel over his shoulder, dark night or not, someone would see him.

It was this idea that caused Drake to avoid the ordinary trails into Mex-town; instead he moved stealthily, trying always to keep something dark and bulky for a background.

He achieved his purpose without incident, and paused in the massive dark shadow of the old Spanish mission to scan southward down through Mex-town.

Candles were burning in the cantina and in one or two other places, but Mex-town's inhabitants customarily retired early, after their late supper. Candlelight was not conducive to much activity after nightfall, at least not vertically, but the abundant crop of local youngsters appeared to attest to some of the horizontal variety.

There were dogs, of course. No Mexican settlement was without its dogs, but their barking, which was frequent day or night, usually aroused little interest. Dogs were kept for a variety of reasons, but after dark their utility was generally confined to routing four-legged night visitors in search of refuse barrels.

Henry listened to the dogs. The ones belonging to inhabitants of the *jacals* nearest the mission were noisily responding to his scent, but not a candle was lighted, no one came outside to investigate. He leaned on his shovel, waiting, listening, and watching. He was nervous but determined, so after a decent interval, feeling safe, he moved stealthily across the front of the massive old mud building and down the near side, where he halted again. This time his heart picked up its cadence a little. He could still look down through Mex-town, but he could also turn his head slightly and see the long *ramada*, with its sagging high overhang and its worn tile paving squares, that ran the full distance of the rear of the mission. Directly eastward, he could see the cemetery, with its rotting wooden headboards and old leaning stone markers. Large old unkempt trees stood among the graves inside a waist-high intricately-made metal fence.

It was too dark to make out details inside the steel fence, but Henry tried to find disturbed earth, indicating the *caja* had been exhumed. All he could be sure of from that distance was two piles of damp soil that were mounded beside freshly dug graves.

He leaned against the rough-worn old wall and waited; he was sweating. The perspiration felt clammy.

He knew the mission priest only casually.

He was a short, dumpy, very dark Mexican. He lived at the mission, and either because he was uncomfortable among gringos or because his English was so bad he was hard to understand, he rarely appeared in Henry's part of town. Henry had heard the man's name, but could not recall it now; nor did he think much about the man, although he was probably the only person who might hear Henry at work with the shovel and come to investigate.

The night was without a breath of stirring air or noticeable movement. The noisy dogs were beginning to slacken their racket. The puny light from the cantina's only window, which faced the plaza, winked out, and someone closed a wooden door. It was impossible to see the proprietor, but the barking told him the man was walking west toward the greatest concentration of adobe residences.

He leaned to be certain the long, dark causeway was empty, as he thought it would be, before leaving the shadows of the massive mud wall.

He had to cross open ground all the way to the cemetery gate, which he eased open very carefully to keep the ancient hinges from grinding and groaning.

Inside, he had some protection among the old ragged trees. He knew from the map approximately where the grave was, and halted against a tree to get his bearings.

The oldest graves had been placed wherever someone wanted to put them, which was mostly close to the big trees for an obvious reason; digging graves was hard, hot work, and the shade mitigated at least part of the heat, especially in summertime.

Henry knew quite a few inhabitants of this place. He recognized several of the markers of the fairly recent deceased.

He worked out the proper area for his digging and walked among the markers to reach that spot. When he saw there was no disturbed earth he was enormously relieved.

It was right here that if Henry had not been excited, somewhat fearful, if his heart hadn't been pounding again, in other words if he had been the shrewd, wary, thoughtful Henry Drake of the store, he would not have been as relieved to find the graves undisturbed as he would have wondered why they hadn't been, since he knew that at least one person, that old, wrinkled *mestizo* with those burning-bright malevolent eyes, knew where his box of money was buried.

He had to figure out which of four graves was the one with the box in it. The map had been specific enough about everything but this, and perhaps its marker had been careless in this regard because *he* knew which grave it was. Henry's problem was compounded by a total lack of sign that recent digging had been done at any of the four graves. Weeds flourished, grass grew, leaves that had fallen over the years to rot seemed not to have been disturbed.

Now it was silent; the dogs had given up, probably bedded down. The crippled moon soared, shadows subtly shifted; the old mission looked even more massive than it was. Henry moved out of the shelter of the trees to stand at the foot of each grave, one at a time, seeking signs of disturbed earth. At the last grave, which bore a very old stone marker from which the lettering had weathered away, he stood a long moment considering the headstone. It had been straightened up very recently.

Henry smiled to himself. He had not relished the idea of having to dig four or more feet to find the box, nor what he knew would be the condition of anyone he encountered at that depth. The freshly stamped earth around the headstone encouraged him to believe his box was probably no more than a foot or two beneath the marker.

As he passed through the weeds on the side of the grave the puny moon slid behind a cloud that had arrived out of nowhere; the sky had been clear when Henry left his house. But the momentary solid darkness did not deter Henry. Neither did the mournful cry of a night bird among the treetops.

He knelt, leaning on the shovel, to squint at the headstone's inscription, but the letters had been irreversibly smoothed out by dozens of winters. He did not really care anyway as he leaned to sift the soil. It was loose but no longer damp. It had clearly been taken up and tamped back into place several days earlier.

Maybe, he told himself, the same day as the robbery by an outlaw Henry was positive had been a Mexican, something Martin Bedford had confirmed for him.

He leaned the shovel aside. This kind of ground he could dig loose with his bare hands.

Before starting to dig he leaned back and looked in all directions. He watched the *ramada* of the old mission for a long time, then turned his back to it and began scooping at the loose dirt.

Once, he almost stopped breathing. At less than six inches he encountered a firm, hard, cold surface. He scratched and dug furiously until he uncovered a large round stone, which he lifted from the hole with a curse and flung aside.

He was breathing hard, so he changed position and rested. In his new position he could watch both the rear of the mission and quite a bit of Mex-town, which was not totally dark. He was facing west with fair visibility to the northwest and southwest. His back was to dozens of grave markers and several big trees.

The soil seemed to be somewhat harder as he dug past the hole where he had removed the rock, but it was moist enough to discourage use of the shovel, which he'd had doubts about using from the moment he'd gotten there. There was no way he could avoid making noise with the shovel. Digging by hand was not entirely noiseless, but the sound traveled no more than the next row or two of graves.

He dug, panted, rested, and dug some more. The ground was still hard but moist. Only when he resumed digging after resting for the third time did it occur to him that the earth he was moving now had not been tamped, had not been disturbed at all. It was probably the same soil the original diggers, perhaps as long as a hundred years ago, had used to fill in the grave.

He rocked back, got back upright, and considered the hole. He wanted to swear at the top of his lungs.

Any other time under different circumstances he would have, but as he stood looking down, sweaty, rumpled, marked by dirt, he did not listen to the silent warning in the back of his brain; he was only conscious of having failed, of having created a hole two feet deep at the expense of torn and bleeding fingernails.

If Henry had met the old wrinkled Mexican at this moment he would have strangled him, and Henry Drake had never been a particularly violent man, had never even aimed a weapon at another human being.

He stood like a stone, looking down. For a time he could almost feel his money and the box it was in, could sense its closeness. That it was not there troubled him in several ways, but primarily, if it was not here, then where was it, for chrissake? It *had* to be here. The little map had been accurate in every way. He had figured it out exactly. Every step he had taken to this spot had been correct right up to these four graves.

He turned to consider the other graves. The moon emerged from behind a vagrant cloud, and five or six seconds after that the reverberation of a gunshot roused half of Mex-town. Henry never heard it.

Echoes chased one another among the old trees, bounced off grave markers and traveled the full length of the *ramada*.

The last echo had died long before any lights appeared in Mex-town. It was not unusual for a householder to shoot a varmint raiding a trash barrel or playing noisy havoc among the maize patches. Some people were not awakened at all, and eventually, because there was only that one gunshot, most of the candles were snuffed out.

It was late, close to midnight. Although the sound had carried, it had not been as loud in the main part of town. Light sleepers over there were unsure whether it had even been a gunshot; they too lay listening before turning onto their sides to go back to sleep.

One man, who was not a particularly light sleeper, emerged from the rear of the old mission holding high a lighted lantern at arm's length. He was short, dumpy, and dark. He was also absolutely certain that what he had heard had been a gunshot. He would even have taken an oath that it was not a handgun. Father Cordero de la Cruz was past sixty, though he was not certain how much past, nor did it matter. He had lost his entire family to *pronunciados* during the innumerable insurrections that he had survived in Mexico. His salvation had been the Holy Church; otherwise he would have hunted down and killed those he thought were responsible for leaving him an orphan. If Father Cordero de la Cruz knew one sound so well he could make distinctions, it was gunfire.

He had also learned long ago never to hold a light of any kind close to his body when there were gunmen in the night.

He walked the length of the old tiled *ramada,* holding the lantern as far out as his arm permitted. At the south end of the sheltered place he scanned Mex-town for activity, but saw none.

He looked in the direction of the gunshot, still with the lantern high and far from his body. There was no sound, no movement. He padded over to the gate of the cemetery, paused to peer before entering, then pushed the gate open and left it open as he started his search. The more time that passed, the more Father Cordero de la Cruz became convinced that whoever had fired a gun in the cemetery was no longer there.

Without a clear idea where the gun had been fired, he padded back and forth among graves and the huge old trees.

It was a time-consuming search, and even after he saw mounded dirt he did not see the body behind it. Except that there was no reason for dirt to be piled near that ancient headstone, he would not have gone for a closer look.

Death was very much a part of life to Father

Cordero de la Cruz. He was surprised but not otherwise perturbed as he moved closer, set the lantern aside, and knelt by the body to feel for signs of life. There were none.

The kneeling priest was able to see something the gloom and shadows had hidden from him before; a raggedly torn shirt with sticky blood that looked black in the gloom. He and *el noche visitador* had met again. The priest knelt close, lowered his head, and prayed first — a fairly long prayer — before he gently rolled the body face up and gasped. He knew the storekeeper, but not well.

The bullet that had killed Henry Drake had come from the front, where the hole was smaller and much less noticeable than where the bullet had exited.

Father Cordero twisted to look in the direction from which the killer had fired. Among the grave markers in that direction was one of the huge old shade trees.

He arose, took the lantern, and walked over there. He felt certain the killer had used the old tree for concealment, and probably as a hand rest before firing, but there was nothing to indicate to the priest that this was so, even though he made a thorough examination of the area for footprints or scuff marks on tree bark.

He returned to the corpse, gently closed

the eyes, said another prayer, picked up his lantern, and walked back to the mission. He was in no hurry; in the chapel with its hauntingly faint scent of incense, an accumulation from over a century of masses, funerals, midnight vigils, and private prayers, he knelt to offer the prayer for the dead. Then he arose, found his hat, and left to tell the gringos what had happened and where they should come to find the body and carry it away.

It was still dark everywhere except along the easterly rim of the world, but people were stirring. In another hour there was more stirring as the little dark priest went among locked stores until he met Jim Rourke sweeping the plankwalk in front of his saloon. Smiling at Rourke, he spoke in labored, disjointed English until Jim leaned aside his broom and held up a hand as he addressed Father Cordero in faultless Mex-Spanish.

The priest was surprised and pleased. In his own language he told the saloonman what had happened, then nodded his head in what almost amounted to a short bow, and walked away, leaving Rourke standing with his mouth open.

7

Jim Rourke's Puzzle

Amid considerable speculation, they buried Henry Drake out where they had buried Ed Ballinger. While those paying last respects were less numerous than they had been for Ballinger's burial, it was still a respectable crowd.

Doc Williams was out there, eyes watering behind thick lenses because the sun was bright, cigar ash down his front as usual. He wore a faintly troubled expression.

After the minister said his prayer for the departed's soul, assuming Henry Drake had one, the men with shovels moved in and the crowd began to disperse.

Doc had been drinking, but because it was an hour or so shy of high noon, and Doc did not begin his serious routine of liquid fortification until about ten in the morning, his head was clear and his voice was strong as he and Jim Rourke stood aside, watching mourners departing in the direction of town.

Doc said, "He's a damned good shot, isn't he."

Rourke nodded. "You think it was the same man?"

"Looks like it, Jim. Each bullet hit squarely through the brisket. Henry's bullet hit dead center, an' it was dark last night."

"How close was he?" Rourke asked.

"I got no idea, except he wasn't very close. There wasn't no scorch or powder burns." Doc twisted to look back where men were shoveling the grave full, his gaze pensive. "I know Henry wouldn't have won no popularity contest, but as far as I know he didn't have the kind of enemies that shot folks."

Rourke, who had been one of the first to locate the corpse, said, "He had a shovel with him. I took it back to town with me. There was a hole near the headstone where he was lying. His hands were dirty — he'd been using them to dig with." The saloonman looked steadily at Doctor Williams. "Why would someone like Henry go to that old mission graveyard an' dig, unless he had good reason to believe there was somethin' buried out there?"

Doc made a guess. "That six hundred dollars he lost to the highwayman?"

Rourke was slow in answering. "What

would make him think his money was buried out there?"

Doc was wearying of this and turned as though to head for town as he said, "All I can say, Jim, is that the Henry Drake I knew wouldn't have been out there in the middle of the night without a damned good reason."

Rourke watched the medical practitioner stride toward town. He and the men filling the grave were all that was left of the folks who had attended the funeral.

Rourke lighted a cigar, trickled smoke, and listened to the steel shovels rattle. Fortunately a man did not have to like a victim to disapprove of murder, which was what Drake's killing had to have been. Although Henry had had a pistol shoved into the waistband of his britches it was still there, unfired and clearly without having been drawn, when the saloonman had arrived at the cemetery.

The priest told him the killer had used either a rifle or a carbine and had shown Rourke where he thought the gunman had fired from.

Rourke strolled back to town, trailing fragrant stogie smoke. He could not shake the feeling that there was something — he could not imagine what — happening according to a plan. By the time he arrived at the saloon, went to his living quarters to shed the celluloid collar and tie, his coat and hat, and changed into something more comfortable and appropriate, he had decided that at the next meeting of the town council he was going to insist a lawman be found and hired, someone with enough experience to maybe sort out this suspicion Rourke had.

It was late afternoon before Jim Rourke had an inspiration that he could not implement until he closed the saloon, but which ate at him until late evening when he decided to clear the place out a tad early, but not without some scowls and tart remarks from customers who had expected to remain until closer to midnight.

At the roominghouse the proprietor told him which room Henry Drake's clerk occupied. Jim rattled the door and traded a level gaze with the younger man when the door opened.

Rourke barged inside without being asked, waited until the door was closed, then said, "Amos, I been wonderin' most of the day why Henry was out yonder with a shovel."

Amos Lawton was in his late twenties and diffident by nature. The clerk went to sit on the edge of his bed as he replied. "I got no idea, but folks that come back from where they found Mister Drake said he was diggin' in a grave." The younger man's eyes wandered. "It don't fit, Mister Rourke. All the time I've known Mister Drake he never seemed to me to be a man who'd try to rob a grave, but he sure acted strange. First he told me he was goin' to eat, then he come back before he'd had time to eat, and rushed into his office . . . Closed the door, which he never did before, an' stayed in there a long time before he come out, told me to lock up, an' left."

"What was he doin' in the office?" Rourke asked.

The clerk frowned faintly at the question. "I got no idea. All I know is that he closed the door an' was in there quite a spell." The clerk's brow creased as he changed the subject in order to clarify something for himself. "Do I keep the store open, or what? I never heard Mister Drake mention havin' any family. Hell, Mister Rourke, this time of year the mercantile does its best business. Folks'll be wanting things, they'll expect the store to be open."

The saloonman said, "Keep the store open. Like you said, folks'll expect that. . . . Amos, did anyone come to the store yesterday or maybe the day before, that Henry waited on — anyone who seemed unusual? Maybe some —"

"There was an old Mexican. Older'n the

hills, raggedy pants, mouth sunk in like he didn't have no teeth. I saw him pay for what he bought with two gold coins. Otherwise Mister Drake waited on the usual run of customers. I was across the room at the glass case where we keep handguns an' pocket watches, but that wrinkled, shriveled old Mexican turned once an' I got to tell you Mister Rourke, his eyes was real bright and fiery looking. They sure didn't go with the rest of him."

Rourke said, "Uh huh, well thanks, Amos."

When Rourke got back out front he rolled his eyes, shook his head, went home, and slept soundly. But when he awakened he decided the old *peon* the clerk mentioned might be worth talking to, not because of his eyes — hell, all Mexicans had dark eyes — but because of the gold coins. Mexicans seldom had gold coins, especially old ones such as the *viejo* the clerk had described.

Rourke was behind his bar, rearranging bottles the following day, when Slade Downing, the local blacksmith, came in. Slade was a thick, powerful bald man who was rarely without a cud of molasses-cured in his cheek. He needed a large glass of beer; he had just finished shoeing three big team-horses for Martin Bedford.

He had run into Doc Williams a little earlier. Doc had told him Bedford was down with the lumbago in his room up at what Slade called "the hotel."

Rourke's voice was inflectionless when he said, "Is that so? How did he catch the lumbago? He never goes out of his office except to eat an' sleep."

The blacksmith knew nothing about that, but it required no brilliance to understand that the saloonman did not care much for Martin Bedford.

Slade paid for his beer and departed. Rourke's next customer was Doc Williams, who did most of his drinking at home; for some reason he seemed to think folks shouldn't see their town medical man in a saloon, which might have been correct if Doc's habit hadn't been common knowledge.

After Rourke got the medical man his jolt and watched him down it, Doc took something from a pocket and spread it atop the bar. It was a crumpled, limp scrap of paper. Jim had to go find his glasses, and when he returned, Doc said, "This was in Henry's pocket. I didn't have time to go through his pants yesterday, so I did it this morning . . . You see that cross?"

"Yes."

"An' that crude sketch of a building below it?"

96

Rourke nodded. "The old mission in Mex-town."

"Yes. Well, now, bend down close and follow out the lines from there to the cemetery . . . Get closer — maybe you'd ought to clean them glasses."

Rourke polished his glasses and almost smiled. For a fact he could see through them much better. He leaned down again, pursed his lips, and frowned. After a while he removed the glasses and stared at Doc Williams. "This was in Henry's pocket?"

Doc nodded and pulled out a blue bandana to wipe his wet eyes.

Rourke considered the worn scrap of paper, which was much less distinct without glasses. "Doc, that leads to the place where Henry got killed."

Again the medical man nodded without speaking as he stowed the bandana, but before the saloonman could speak again, Doc asked a question. "Didn't you tell me yesterday you brought back a shovel from out there?"

"Yes . . . Well I'll be damned! Buried treasure?"

"That'd fit, wouldn't it? Henry more'n likely never used a shovel in his life, so it had to be somethin' real worthwhile for him to go out yonder with one, wouldn't it?"

Jim Rourke had already passed that point

in the mystery. He said, "Where did Henry get that little map?"

Doc Williams said nothing.

They gazed at each other for a long moment before Rourke hooked his glasses back into place and bent down. Doc Williams's watery gaze ranged along the backbar with its assortment of bottles. He cleared his throat, and when Rourke looked up, Doc pushed the sticky little jolt glass forward without a word.

After Doc had dropped his whiskey straight down, the saloonman said, "If that's what Henry was doin' out there I'd like to know where he got this piece of paper." An abrupt idea came to Jim Rourke. If someone had given the map to Henry at the store, possibly the clerk might have seen the transaction. But he had to wait hours before he could go up to the roominghouse again.

He did not close the saloon until almost eleven o'clock, by which time his clientele had thinned out considerably. He told the hangers-on the bar was closed and watched them depart too, taking their time. It was amazing how long it took men to drink beer when an observer was getting more impatient by the minute.

This time the clerk was bedded down when Rourke rattled his door, and this time, too, the younger man seemed less than enchanted when he recognized his visitor. He pointed to a chair and perched on the side of his bed as the saloonman asked if he had seen the old Mexican give a piece of paper to Mister Drake before leaving the store.

Before replying, the clerk yawned mightily. "All I saw was Mister Drake pick up somethin' off the floor and go toward the trash barrel with it, stop, study the piece of paper, then go behind the counter and smooth it out. I figured someone had maybe dropped a letter. Mister Drake never mentioned the piece of paper, so naturally, neither did I."

"You got any idea what was on that piece of paper?"

"Not even a good guess. After he'd smoothed it out an' studied it a minute or so, he took the paper with him an' headed for his office."

"Amos, was that right after the old beaner left the store?"

"Well, maybe a little later'n that."

"But he was Henry's last customer of the day?"

"Yes . . . He said he was goin' to supper, for me to lock up. That struck me as odd because ever since I've worked for him, he almost always locks the door himself, an' this time he told me to lock up."

"Did the old Mexican come back lookin' for the paper he'd dropped?"

"No, an' I'd have known if he had because I was the only one left in the store."

Rourke arose to depart, but the younger man's gaze was fixed on him. "Is there somethin' goin' on, Mister Rourke?"

The older man smiled as he walked toward the door. "Your guess is as good as mine, partner. Sorry I rousted you out of bed."

It was much too late to go down to Mextown, so Rourke returned to the saloon and went to bed in his storeroom behind the saloon. But he did not sleep very well, even after telling himself he wasn't a detective; that although it looked like the old man had accidentally dropped the piece of paper, since it seemed to reveal the hiding place of some kind of treasure, sure as hell the old man had known what was written on the paper, and knowing that he would have returned to the store to look for the paper.

Maybe not; old men were notorious for forgetting things, but one thing Rourke intended to do the following day was hunt down that old Mexican.

The following morning, after Rourke opened his saloon and was sweeping the floor, he stopped stone-still in the center of the big, rank-smelling room. He recalled that Henry had asked the meaning of that Spanish word, and had acted downright fidgety when Rourke had explained what it meant. At the time Rourke had harbored uncharitable thoughts about Henry Drake, because gun-running and smuggling were lucrative enterprises and Henry had never been an individual to overlook an opportunity to make money. Even though Drake had acted shocked, even outraged, when Rourke had mentioned peddling or receiving contraband, that word was on the little map and Drake had had the map in his pants pocket when he was killed. After asking what the word meant, he had taken a shovel and gone out where the map indicated — and someone was sure as hell waiting for him.

Jim Rourke was routed from his reverie by the arrival of Martin Bedford, who nodded, went to the bar, and called for some beer. Rourke filled the glass and took it down the bar. He watched the stage company's man down it while trying to recall if he'd ever served Bedford beer this early in the day before.

Bedford put the empty glass aside and leaned on the counter, looking directly at Jim Rourke. "I was just up at Doc's place gettin' a boil lanced," he said, without letting his eyes drift from the saloonman's face. "He showed me that little piece of paper Henry'd been carrying in a pocket. He said the two of you figured out the map on that paper was what you'n him figured got Henry to go up yonder last night."

Rourke nodded. "That's about the size of it."

"Well, he didn't find a box, did he?"

"Don't seem that he did. Why?"

"Walt Bellamy come in last night from the north run. He was ahead of schedule — for a damned change — and when he come to the place where that highwayman robbed him, it being fresh in his mind, he stopped the coach and went pokin' around back up in the trees an' underbrush. He found Henry's little steel-bound money box an' brought it back to town with him."

The disagreeable man smiled without a shred of mirth. "The money was gone, of course, an' the lock had been shot off, so it seems that if what you'n Doc figured out about Henry goin' to the old Mex graveyard was because he thought his box an' money was buried up there, you was wrong, wouldn't you say?"

Jim Rourke had never liked the stage company man, and right now Bedford's patronizing attitude had him boiling. "The box was

102

empty, wasn't it?"

"Yes."

"Well, there wasn't anythin' buried up there, but if there had been it couldn't have been in the box, could it?"

"No."

"But the map said *caja*. You know what that means?"

"Yes, I asked my Mex yardman, it means box. What of it — the damned box wasn't up there."

"But Henry didn't know that, did he? Not if Walt only found the box last night? So he thought sure as hell his box of money was buried up there."

For a moment Bedford was silent, but as he raised up off the bar the words came. "An' you think *caja* was put on the map to trick Henry into goin' up yonder to dig up his box?"

Rourke nodded slowly. "I think it sure looks like it, Martin, an' I'll tell you somethin' else. Whoever shot Henry was most likely waitin' up there for him, just like they was lyin' in wait down yonder for Ed Ballinger."

The stage company man straightened up and tapped a couple of times with his fingers, then threw a cold smile in Jim Rourke's direction as he walked out of the saloon without another word.

8

A Cold Snap

It was a nice day but with masses of clouds hovering just beyond and above the distant northerly mountains. The sun was warm. Except for the threat in those clouds, the Anasazi Pueblo was bathed in soft light with some shadows, oblivious to any threat.

The range for miles in all directions had grass and cattle, mostly a long way from the wide arroyo and its prehistoric ruins.

When Martin Bedford rode down one of the trails, he left the footing up to the horse. He was concentrating on a thoroughbred-looking big horse and the individual who owned such a horse.

He was there, this time perched on an eroded mud wall that had at one time been much taller, and he had seen Bedford the moment he left the mesa to descend.

There were larks in the grass, some white-tailed deer watering at a tiny creek. The birds fled first, then the deer, as the rider rode directly toward the man sitting on the old mud wall.

Martin Bedford drew rein, nodded, got a nod back, and wasted no time on preliminaries. "The feller who runs the saloon an' the town doctor got a scrap of paper with a map on it that pointed the way to the spot where Henry Drake was killed."

The man with tawny-brown eyes and a slightly hawkish cast to his tanned face smiled and said nothing. Bedford began to scowl and sounded testy as he said, "They got it figured out, Mister Halcón."

Halcón continued to smile. "They may have figured out Drake was pulled to the cemetery by the map, and they know that's where he was killed, but they don't know anything else, do they?"

Martin dismounted and stood beside his horse. He did not like the other man's unconcern, which, if Rourke and Doc kept on figuring, might lead back to him.

"Mister Halcón, the old Mex told me you took care of things."

"I do."

"Well, don't it worry you that two men in town are gettin' uncomfortably close?"

"No."

"It worries me, Mister Halcón."

The man perching on the mud wall still

105

smiled as he held out a hand, palm up.

Martin Bedford stared. He understood perfectly what that extended hand meant, but he had not ridden out here to pay for more murder; in fact he did not have more than forty dollars in his pocket. He raised his eyes. The smiling man said, "It's your worry, Mister Bedford, not mine."

Bedford stood stone-still, glaring. Anger came slowly but solidly. Along with it came a sickening realization that when he had hired Halcón to kill Henry Drake, he had put himself at his mercy.

"I don't have that much money with me," he told the hired killer, who slowly drew his arm back, placed his hand back atop the eroded mud wall, and considered Martin Bedford while his smile faded.

Eventually Halcón said, "I could ride back with you and wait outside town until you get the money. I'm used to waiting, Mister Bedford."

A vein in Martin Bedford's neck swelled and pulsed. He was armed, but he quivered at the idea of a hired killer.

Halcón spoke again, enunciating very clearly. "Six hundred dollars isn't too much to pay to stop the doctor and the saloonman from getting any closer to you, is it?"

Bedford's face was splotchy red. He looked

unblinkingly at the other man, who gazed back the same way. Eventually the stage company man said, "I can get you three hundred dollars, but that's all."

Halcón replied quietly, "Mister Bedford, in my business we don't horse-trade. No cut rates, no promises, just cash."

Martin flung around, swung back astride, glared, spun his horse, and rode up out of the arroyo. He reined back toward Calabasas stiff with fury.

It was a long ride; men with a reason to think had plenty of time to do it in eighteen miles. By the time Martin Bedford had rooftops in sight, evening was descending, the fragrance of supper fires was abroad, and he had calmed down; not a whole lot, but enough to have worked out a solution to his dilemma.

The lantern was alight atop its pole as he entered the corralyard, but since no stage would be leaving until daybreak he saw no one as he cared for the horse, went to his office, lighted a lamp, hurled his hat at the rack, and dropped down on his desk chair.

A calmer individual would have traced his situation back to the killing of Henry Drake and would have heartily regretted ever having sponsored it, but Martin Bedford was never entirely calm, even when he was asleep. Right now, if he'd known how to go about it, he would have paid three hundred dollars to someone to kill Halcón. But that was not his real cause for anxiety; a hired killer could be shot for revenge, but revenge was not Martin Bedford's problem.

The problem was Jim Rourke and that cussed old sot of a medical doctor. He sat a long while in thought. When he finally blew down the mantle to douse the lamp, he had just about embraced an idea he did not like at all, and wouldn't have normally considered because, surly, disagreeable, and mean as he was, he had never shot a man in his life, let alone two men.

That night a cold, fitful wind arrived, and until daylight no one knew it presaged the advance of mile-high clouds that were massed together while moving with ponderous, inexorable slowness in the direction of the Calabasas country.

The wind had passed by sunup, but in its wake arrived an unseasonably chilly cold front. People went hurriedly to place brown paper bags over sprouting tomato and bean plants. They wanted at all costs to avoid losing their vegetable patches again, because it was almost too late to start over.

Some sprouts could survive a black frost, but they were the varieties of vegetables no one cared to exist on through a harsh winter. One was rhubarb, another was seemingly endless varieties of squash.

Walt Bellamy appeared at the saloon, swaddled inside his old sheep-pelt coat and still wearing his gauntlets. His nose was cold and his eyes were watering as he removed the gloves, shook his head at Jim Rourke, and waited for the bottle and glass to be set up. "Son-of-a-bitching country," he said. "If a man had the sense gawd gave a goose he'd ride south from here an' never look back."

Rourke jerked his head in the direction of the big cast-iron cannon heater he'd fired up first thing that morning, and as the disgruntled stage driver crossed toward the stove with his whiskey, Rourke said, "Damned unusual this late in the year, Walt."

Bellamy would not be placated. As he stood wide-legged with his back to the stove he snarled a reply. "Like hell, Jim. I've seen these cold snaps hit a hunnert times in the last fifteen years." Bellamy downed his whiskey, coughed, dashed water from his eyes, and breathed deeply before speaking again. "I busted my butt buckin' wind since midnight, tryin' to keep the horses' heads up, just to make time and arrive in the yard on schedule, an' you know what? Martin jumped all over me, chewed me up one side an' down the other."

"If you was on schedule, why did he do that?"

Walt returned to the bar to refill his little glass before answering. "For no damned reason at all. Since when does Martin need a reason to be mean? He was born mean. Someone must've beat him over the head with a mean stick before he was dry . . . No damned reason at all."

Bellamy downed his second jolt, his face got decent color; his eyes still watered but part of that could have been the result of driving into the wind half the night. He got comfortable enough to loosen his coat. When Jim went to refill the jolt glass again Walt put a thick hand over it. Two was all he ever had after coming in from a run.

"Something's eating him," he said to Rourke. "I've known Martin six years, since I first hired on. I've seen him mad a lot of times. Even when he's in a good mood he cusses at the horses, at the yardmen, at the drivers. But this time it was different. Somethin' eatin' on him, but I got no idea what it is . . . For a plugged *centavo* I'd quit."

"Walt, you're the only good driver he's got. The others come an' go like birds."

"Yes, an' you know why, too, don't you?

You don't like him either. Don't tell me different, I've seen the way you look at him. Y'know, Jim, it's always puzzled me why someone he jumps on, like he done to me a while back, don't shoot him."

Rourke smiled without a shred of humor. "It could still happen. Be patient."

Liveryman Alex Jobey came in accompanied by Slade Downing, the blacksmith. Both wore coats and hats. Alex even had gloves on. They nodded to Walt and called for a bottle and two glasses. Before Rourke could serve them they both started growling about the abrupt change in the weather.

Alex, who was the oldest man in the room, squinted at the others and said something that made them all stare at him in silence.

"The Indians cause these changes. When I was young I lived four years with the Crow. They had a medicine man who could make rain, hot weather, even wind. He was best at makin' wind. One time he dang near got himself killed; a big wind come up and blew over half the tipis. He an' I was sound asleep when some bucks come in, dragged him outside, and beat the hell out of him." Alex nodded soberly. "He told me afterward he hadn't really caused that damned big wind, but that's what he was dreamin' about when it come."

Walt Bellamy cleared his throat. Jim got busy behind the bar, and the blacksmith looked down his nose at Alex but said nothing.

The raffish liveryman scowled at them. "You think I'm makin' this up? Well, let me tell you — I've stood right there an' seen some of 'em do things you'd never believe.

"I knew an old Indian called Shahaka. He wasn't Crow. He lived with the band, but he come from off in the northwest somewhere. He was Mandan. He told us his tribe was wiped out by smallpox, an' he didn't want to talk 'bout it. The old screwt — now you don't have to believe this — that old screwt could conjure."

Rourke frowned. "He could what?"

"Conjure. It means he could talk to spirits — he could conjure them folks up. I've sat right there when he'd conjure. I could hear the spirit talkin' an' the old man answerin'."

Walt Bellamy snorted like a horse.

Alex bristled. "I told you you wouldn't believe. Listen — I was right there in the hide house when old Shahaka conjured the devil one time. There was a lodge full of Crows an' me."

This was too much; Walt turned toward the liveryman. "This old tomahawk talked to the devil? I expect you're goin' to say you saw him."

"I *heard* him, Walt, as plain as I heard you just now."

"Is that so? An' what did he say?"

"He told Shahaka he wouldn't make no smallpox epidemic wipe out the soldiers at the fort because if he did, the epidemic would spread to the Mandans an' kill them all too. Old Shahaka told the devil he'd have the Mandans move far off. He said — everyone in the lodge that night heard this — the Devil said all right, but the Mandans would have to move off so far they'd be lost."

"Well?" demanded Walt Bellamy.

"Well," the liveryman replied quietly. "Something went wrong. The epidemic killed all the Mandans an' never took hold among the soldiers. Only old Shahaka come through an' a few others. They run him off; they tried to find him an' kill him, but he outfigured 'em."

Jim Rourke said dryly, "I'd want to kill him, too. Seems to me your old medicine man wasn't too good at his trade."

Slade Downing was uncomfortable. He'd agreed to come up here with Alex Jobey for a drink, not to be associated with someone who'd tell all that hogwash.

The blacksmith distanced himself from the

liveryman; he moved to the far end of the bar where Walt Bellamy was, leaned over, and exchanged a look with the coach driver while he wagged his head.

Alex was stung by the unanimous scorn of his acquaintances. He slammed money atop the bar for his liquor and stamped as far as the door before he turned, raked them all with a fierce look, and made a parting remark. "An' here's something else you can stuff in your pipes and smoke it! I heard the devil laugh. *Twice.*"

After the liveryman's departure there was a long, uncomfortable silence. Jim Rourke broke it by offering to stand the next round.

Walt Bellamy departed. Across the road there was no light in Mister Bedford's office. Walt crossed over, traversed the full length of the corralyard to reach the bunkhouse, and bedded down with wind scrabbling along the lodgepole eaves.

Calabasas slept, the wind howled, and along toward morning a few pats of rain jerked dust to life in the roadway, but for all the menace of the cloud galleons directly overhead, it did not rain more than a trace amount.

Folks said the wind was responsible for driving the clouds westerly. Out there where range stockmen needed every drop of summertime rain they could get, the clouds dumped their load.

The air smelled of rain and the cold persisted, but it did not get below freezing, which was a great cause of relief among all folks who had vegetable gardens.

The new day arrived, the sun began its climb, and by midday there was warmth again and no wind.

Walt Bellamy crossed to the cafe for breakfast. The place was crowded, noisy, and steamy, which was invariably the case early mornings; single men and a few who were not single kept the cafeman hopping like a kitten on a hot tin roof.

Martin Bedford was not among the diners, which pleased his driver, but it also stuck in the back of Bellamy's mind that this was, as nearly as he could recall, the first time Martin hadn't been among the cafeman's first customers of the day.

9
"Mister Rourke!"

Three days after the wind and those threatening clouds had passed, Jim Rourke went out to the back alley to put some empties in the trash barrel and paused to scan the sky; this had been the damnedest summer he'd seen since he'd been in the Calabasas country, and it wasn't over yet.

The sky was soft blue and clear from horizon to horizon. Jim felt reassured; it was time, for gawd's sake, for real summer to arrive.

He turned to go back inside, caught a furtive movement nearly opposite, and twisted to look at the same time a big dog barked excitedly beyond an old board fence.

Jim turned to face fully around. It was probably a cat, of which Calabasas had its share that never seemed to go very far from the trash barrels.

He saw nothing, left the dog to his barking, slammed the door, and went back inside. As he closed the door, the dog had another barking fit, but Jim Rourke didn't pay any attention.

An hour later he was attracted to the roadway by someone yelling. Others, attracted by the noise, were looking northward. Doc Williams' top buggy was approaching from the north at a plodding walk, the lines dragging in the dust. Doc was slumped half over the dashboard.

The harness maker, Jem Dugan, a thin, wrinkled old man ran out to stop the horse. Others came up, but Jim remained where he was. His first hunch was that John Barleycorn had finally caught up with Doc, but Dugan loudly said, "He's been shot! Couple you lads give me a hand an' we'll tote him home."

A buxom graying woman protested. "There's no one at his house to look after him."

Martin Bedford replied waspishly to the woman. "If he ain't dead he's close to it. Take him up to the roominghouse — folks can look after him there."

Jim Rourke called to Bedford. "Shot?"

Bedford turned his head. "There's blood all over. He's been shot for a fact."

"Who in hell would shoot — ?"

"How would I know?" Bedford exclaimed, and turned to help lift Doc out of the rig.

Jim heard him say, "Looks like some-one's been butcherin' hawgs in this buggy . . . Be careful . . . Yeah, I know he's heavy . . . Couple more of you gents lend us a hand."

The crowd was increasing by the minute, and there was little conversation as they carried Doc up to the roominghouse. The proprietor met them at the porch and told them to walk slow, he had to get a rubber blanket or Doc was going to ruin the bedding.

Rourke watched until they had Doc inside, then turned to go back in the saloon. Slade Downing was there, puffing hard. He had run all the way from the lower end of town, where his smithy was located.

Jim started to tell him what had happened, but the look on the burly bald man's face stopped him. The blacksmith spoke slowly. "I was out back an' heard the gunshot . . . Jim, I seen you duckin' back into the saloon."

Rourke's eyes widened. "He was in his rig north of town, Slade, an' I didn't hear anything. Sure I was out back dumpin' junk in the trash barrel. What of it?"

Downing walked in the direction of the roominghouse without another word. Jim watched him go, completely baffled.

Later, a tad shy of high noon, half-deaf Pete Bradley from the poolhall came in for a glass of beer and soberly watched Rourke's every move as he filled the glass. When he set it up, the only patron in the saloon sipped thoughtfully while gazing steadily at Jim. Rourke broke the silence. "Have you been up there? Is he still alive?"

Bradley counted out some coins, placed them beside his empty glass, looked at Jim for a moment, then walked out of the saloon without having uttered a word.

Later, several of the townsmen who had carried Doc up to the roominghouse came in, got drinks, and looked at Jim from solemn faces. He had a bad feeling as he said, "Did he make it?"

One man replied, his voice like ice. "He's the doctor, Jim. Maybe he could say whether he will or not, but to me he looked like he'd be lucky to see the sunset."

Rourke looked from man to man. "What the hell is wrong with you fellers?"

Another, younger, man, a rider for one of the cow outfits who had come to town for the mail, fixed Jim with a dark look and said nothing until he'd emptied his beer glass, then, as he set it down, he spoke in the same cold tone of voice. "Wasn't you the one at the meetin' of the town council who was against hirin' a replacement for Marshal Ballinger?"

Rourke stared at the rangeman. "Who told you that? What I said was we'd ought to choose the next lawman real careful."

The rangeman's black eyes did not blink. "Tell me somethin', Jim — was you out of the saloon this morning?"

Rourke was sweating. "Long enough to dump trash in the barrel in the alley . . . What the hell is wrong with you fellers?"

"Someone snuck up the back alley, set half the dogs in town to caterwaulin'. . . . Slade said you told him you didn't hear a gunshot."

"That's right. I didn't."

"Well, most other folks did. . . . I was ridin' into town from the west side. I heard the shot, an' Doc's rig was ahead of me, just comin' into town from the north . . . The shot came from the other side, easterly, about at the upper end of the alley on your side."

Rourke's sick feeling increased. He stared from man to man. Except for the cowboy, he knew every one of them, had known them for a long time. He leaned against the shelf at his back. They were watching him from closed faces, even those among them who had been his friends. They were regarding him the same way Slade Downing had, without clear hostility, but with hard stares and expressionless faces.

He could not believe any of this. It was too unbelievable. One of the townsmen spoke quietly. "Doc was shot in the left side, Jim. That's the same direction you was in when you left the saloon to go out into the alley."

Rourke's heart was barely beating. He had lived a hard, rough life, had faced his share of peril, but this was the first time he had ever felt as he felt now. *They believed he had shot Doc Williams.*

He crossed both arms over his chest. "Why would I do anythin' like that?"

The rangeman said, "You tell us. Someone said you was real interested in the store-keeper's murder — you asked a lot of questions. They said you was the first one up at the cemetery an' you brought back a shovel from up there."

"I did. I brought the shovel back. It's in my shed. What of it?"

A heavyset older man spoke next. "What else did you bring back, Jim?"

"What else? Nothin', for cris'sake! Not a damn thing."

"Why did you bring the shovel back?"

"Well . . . why not? If it was left up there someone else would take it, wouldn't they?" He paused, scarcely breathing. He was defensive; even to himself he did not sound convincing. He had been baffled and upset, but now he also felt a cold chill of fear. He uncrossed his arms as he addressed them again.

"I didn't know Doc was out of town. We talked yesterday right here in the saloon. He had a couple of jolts. When he left he —"

"He what?" the heavyset man asked.

"Well, we'd been talkin' about Henry and Ed gettin' killed. Henry mostly. Doc showed me a piece of old paper with a little map on it. We figured from the map there was somethin' buried at the old Mex cemetery. Maybe Henry's money box that was taken off the stage by that highwayman some time back. That's all; we talked an' Doc left."

"Do you have that piece of paper?" the heavyset man asked.

Jim shook his head. "It was Doc's, he'd found it in Henry's pocket. He took it with him."

An older man bored Jim with a cold stare. "But you memorized the map, Jim, an' what I'm thinkin' right now is that — How much money was in Henry's box?"

"I don't know."

"But it would be a sizable amount, wouldn't it? An' after Doc left, seems to me you got to figurin' that with Doc dead only you'd know, so you —"

"Wait a minute," Rourke exclaimed.

122

"There was no box up there. Most of you had ought to know that. Some of you was up there, too. You saw where Henry had dug, an' there wasn't a box, was there?"

The heavyset man replied softly. "None of us got up there before you did, Jim. You was the first one. We didn't even know you'd taken the shovel until much later . . . *if* that's all you took from up there."

Those last eight words fell into the silence like stones. Rourke pushed sweat off his forehead with a sleeve. The townsmen left the rangerider behind and departed. The cowboy went to a chair, swung it so that he could watch Rourke, pulled out his clasp knife, and went to whittling on a scrap of wood that had been atop a nearby table. He occasionally glanced up. He had the blackest eyes Jim had ever seen, and while he had long ago ceased trying to remember all the seasonal riders who patronized the saloon during the riding season, he was certain he had never seen this cowboy before.

It was very quiet, not only in the saloon but outside as well. Normally, at this time of day there would be people on the plankwalks, riders passing, occasionally a wagon or a buggy.

Jim got himself a drink and held the bottle aloft. The rangeman shook his head and went back to whittling.

Several blue-tailed flies were battering themselves against a front window, which was by no means uncommon, even in wintertime, except that the other times they could be seen but not heard. Today, their noise reached all the way back to the bar as Jim Rourke leaned with both arms atop the counter, staring into space.

Alone with the intransigent rangeman he could almost forget his friends staring at him from across the bar. Almost.

He went back over the questions they had asked and his answers. He remembered the blank faces, the stances, the clear evidence in their attitude that they had believed rumors, guesses, spite talk. And he had not heard a damned gunshot, which bothered him because if Doc had been bushwhacked at the north end of town by someone in town, why hadn't he heard the muzzleblast?

He thought back over everything he had done, and remembered what had seemed to be furtive movement passing beyond the old fence toward the north end of the alley. He remembered following the sound of barking dogs and thinking that whatever he had glimpsed had been creeping toward the upper end of the alley.

The cowboy interrupted Rourke's reverie.

124

"Mister, you're in a peck of trouble, an' I'd take it kindly if you'd stay right where you are."

Jim nodded; it had not occurred to him not to stand where he was. He shook his head in the rangeman's direction. "They can't honestly believe I shot Doc, can they?"

"Yep, they can. That business of a box of greenbacks bein' hid an' Mister Drake goin' after it is the only thing that sticks in my craw." The cowboy paused long enough to hoist both booted feet to the tabletop and lean back. He looked straight at Rourke. "Why would a highwayman who had just raided a stage ride south to the town where the coach was headed to bury his loot? I wouldn't have. I'd have rode in the opposite direction an' never stopped until I was too tuckered to go on."

Rourke, who was thoroughly familiar with rangemen, since half or more of his customers were from outlying cattle outfits, began to feel just barely hopeful. "Neither would anyone else in his right mind," he stated, agreeing with the rangeman.

The cowboy smiled. "Unless he figured Calabasas would be the last place possemen would look for him."

Jim scowled. "There wasn't a posse."

The cowboy went silent and remained that

125

way for a long while, and although his gaze drifted, it never left Rourke for more than moments. He warned Jim just once.

"If you got a sawed-off gun under the bar, don't make a move to reach for it, will you?"

Rourke moved his eyes in a different direction without answering.

As he grew calmer he thought back: they had arrived at the saloon the way men would who more than half believed what they had heard or had assumed, their purpose to listen to Jim and make their final judgment according to what he said. Right now, he had a feeling he had just about dug his own grave with them.

He had another jolt and put the bottle back on its shelf. It was still incredible; he knew those men, had known them for years. They knew he and Doc had always got along.

The cowboy spoke quietly from his tipped-back chair. "Why didn't you catch him out somewhere, if you was dead set on shootin' him?"

Rourke studied the prematurely lined face with its heavy jaw and square chin. Talking to the rangeman, trying to reason with him, would be like talking to a stone wall. He did not answer, so the cowboy went back to whittling.

Those blue-tailed flies were still beating

126

against the window. Somewhere at the lower end of town a horse squealed and immediately after that someone, most likely Slade Downing or his apprentice, began warping hot steel over an anvil.

Enos Jordan, the livery barn hostler, came in, nodded pleasantly, looked at the cowboy, and leaned on the bar as he asked for a jolt. Jim got him what he wanted. Enos offered a little salute to Jim and downed the whiskey. Within moments his face got good color, his lanky frame straightened, his eyes were brighter, and he smiled as he put silver atop the bar and nodded for a refill, which Jim supplied with the rangeman watching them both. This time, after the hostler threw back his head and swallowed just once, he expelled a loud breath, raised a filthy cuff to his eyes, and shook his head.

Rourke took the small glass and dropped it into his bucket of greasy water, which signaled that he would not serve Enos more liquor.

The hostler smiled slightly; he was accustomed to folks making decisions about him, and for him. He said, "The town's full of talk, Mister Rourke."

Jim nodded dourly. "I expect it is."

"Well — you know what they're saying?"

"I can guess, Enos."

"But you never done it, did you?"

"No."

The lanky thin man leaned off the bar, looking pleased with himself. "That's what I been saying. Mister Rourke'd never shoot Doc Williams. Why hell, they was such good friends they both peed through the same knothole."

Jim sighed. "Alex'll be wonderin' where you are."

The hostler nodded, turned, and marched out of the saloon. The cowboy snapped his knife closed, pocketed it, and gave Rourke a quizzical look. "He dungs out down at the livery barn," Rourke said with a shrug. "He's killin' himself with whiskey. Folks figure he was born with one foot out of the stirrups."

The cowboy relaxed. "Well, you got a friend," he said.

Rourke thought about that. He needed more than one friend; he needed lots of friends right now. "Yeah, I guess so," he told the cowboy.

10

More Questions than Answers

The afternoon waned, shadows lengthened; there was both foot and hoof traffic again. Jim leaned on his bartop, waiting, but none of his regulars arrived.

The cowboy seemed to have infinite patience. Jim wondered which cow outfit he worked for and how much time he could waste before he had to head back.

None of this appeared to bother the rider. He had finished whittling and now sat slumped, gazing at nothing, but with Rourke visible from the corner of his eyes.

The waiting was abruptly broken when Martin Bedford, Jem Dugan, and Slade Downing entered from the back alley. They ignored Jim as they went around in front of the bar and settled there. The turkey-necked harness maker jerked his head at the cowboy. "We're real obliged, partner. From

129

here on we'll mind things if you got to get back."

The rider arose, gazed a little pensively at Jim Rourke, nodded to everyone, and departed.

Martin Bedford's expression was always cynical, but now it was also menacing as he leaned on the bar. "You went out in the alley to dump trash in the barrel, is that right, Jim?"

"I already said that. Yes, that's right!"

"What'd you dump in the barrel?"

"Empty bottles, some sweepings . . . What the hell do you think you're doing?"

Slade Downing answered. "We're trying to figure who shot Doc. Everyone in town's got an interest in it, Jim. Doc died an hour or so ago. Does that make you feel good?"

Rourke reddened; he leaned on the bar with his right hand below where his twelve-gauge scattergun rested. He was angry. Few people had ever seen Rourke's temper, but he had one.

He looked from one of the men across the bar to the others. When he spoke, he glared straight at the only man among them he had never liked.

"This has gone on long enough. You sons of bitches get it through your thick skulls once an' for all. *I did not shoot Doc!* You understand that?"

They took being called a fighting name without showing resentment, but their closed faces showed nothing anyway. The oldest among them, Jem Dugan, was about to speak when Martin Bedford held up his left hand for silence, brought up his right hand, and placed a length of new rope atop the counter. The hangknot part of the rope had been tied by an experienced hand. Bedford said, "Ever seen this before, Jim?"

Rourke's shock passed. He looked the stage company's man in the eye and said, "Never in my damned life!"

"Well, now," stated Bedford in a soft, slow tone as though he relished each word, "maybe you can tell us how it got in your trash barrel in the alley."

Jim was speechless as he stared at the rope. It had been cut off about a foot and a half above the knot. He said, "I never saw that thing before in my life."

The silence drew out and thickened until someone came through the spindle doors from the late-day road. Everyone turned and at least some of the men at the bar did not welcome the newcomer, whoever he was.

It was the mercantile's clerk, Amos Lawton, whose colorless personality had never made much of an impression.

He did not understand that he had intruded

until it registered that Jim Rourke and the men across from Jim were staring at him, by which time the clerk was nearly at the bar. He smiled feebly, nodded, and deferentially asked for a glass of beer.

Martin Bedford snarled, "We're holdin' a private meetin' here. We don't need no onlookers, so get your damned butt out of here!"

The clerk winced, and his eyes moved in several directions as Rourke said, "Stay where you are. I'll get you a beer."

The clerk seemed willing to leave. Jim's gruff tone, which might have encouraged hesitation in someone else, had the opposite effect on the store clerk. He kept smiling timidly, teetering with indecision, until he saw something that changed him completely.

He jutted his chin. "That's it. That's the rope I sold a rangeman the day Mister Ballinger was killed."

Only the sound of Rourke drawing off a beer was audible. Jim slammed the full glass in front of the clerk and stood, glaring at his accusers.

Martin Bedford had a question. "Are you plumb sure this here is the same rope?"

"I'm sure, Mister Bedford. That's not lasso rope, that's binder rope." The clerk drained half his beer and put the glass aside. They were staring at him, so he told them the rest of it.

"I don't know whether any of you gents remember a sort of coppery-brown rangeman with sort of tan-red eyes who'd been around a few days some time back. He come to the store for supplies an' bought a length of that rope."

Martin Bedford went to a chair and sat down. He turned the chair so he could not see the rope or the other men.

The others ignored Bedford. Slade Downing asked the store clerk if he was plumb positive the rope atop the bar was the same rope.

The clerk's reply made Rourke want to smile. "Mister Downing, it's the same rope off the same coil I cut it from. An' that rangeman's the only person to buy any of that rope in six months. *That is the same rope!*"

Jim Rourke snarled, "I never dumped no rope in my trash barrel." As his angry eyes fixed on the silent men before him, he continued, "Now then — if someone put that rope in my barrel, an' since you three found it there, just tell me: How did you happen to be lookin' in my trash barrel? An' which one of you put the rope in there?"

The consternation was visible as the blacksmith and the harness maker looked at each other. Martin Bedford rose abruptly and walked out of the saloon. With that example, so did the other two accusers.

Rourke picked up the rope, slid the knot up and down, and said, "He sure knew how to make a slip knot, didn't he?"

The clerk had finished his beer and was thinking of something else. Something that made him very uncomfortable. "I wondered at the time . . . We've had that coil of rope for more'n a year. We sold off some to a freighter last spring, otherwise . . . Mister Rourke, why would a rangeman need heavy rope like that? I wondered when he bought it."

Jim didn't answer the question, he asked one. "Who was that rider?"

"I don't know, but I recall seein' him a time or two around town. I saw him come in here one time."

Rourke's expression hardened. "Pleasant feller, was he? Looked to be maybe half Mex or Indian?"

"Yes. An' polite. An' he paid with a gold coin." The clerk gazed at Jim. "Only other time we've taken in gold for a long time was from that old Mexican. That was about the time the rangeman paid in gold for the rope."

Rourke sought his backbar stool and sat

on it. He remembered that cowboy, remembered idly wondering whether he was part Mexican or part Indian. He recalled their casual conversation, found nothing unusual about it, and went to refill the clerk's glass, and to draw off a beer for himself.

They were quiet for a long time, both thinking back, both beginning to feel uneasy, when the little priest from Mex-town walked in, smiled all the way up to the bar, and spoke in Spanish to the only man he knew in Calabasas who spoke Spanish like a native. As he began to speak in Spanish, the store clerk looked bewildered. He muttered thanks for the beer and departed.

Father Cordero de la Cruz declined Rourke's offer of a drink and spoke in an almost solemn tone. "I am sorry to know the doctor is dead. Of his kind there are never enough, don't you agree?"

Rourke agreed. *"Nunca, Padre."*

The priest cleared his throat as he glanced around the empty room. "We are alone, no?"

"Sí, padre, solo!"

The white segment of the priest's eyes were brownish, almost the color of mud. His gaze at Rourke was fixed. He was clearly troubled and delayed what he had to say next until Rourke wondered if he was going to speak at all.

135

He spoke. "I worry, my friend. Always there is danger in this life, in this world, especially when one does not understand. You comprehend?"

Rourke smiled. "Yes, Father, I understand."

"Pay attention, listen to me. This morning early an old man came to me. He would not come inside the church, but wanted to say something to me on the porch . . . I've seen him but have no knowledge of him. He has no teeth, and although he appears to be very old his eyes almost look through you when he talks."

"He had a name, Father?"

"I don't know but I will find out . . . He said to me a man in Gringo-town was being stalked by another man with a gun, and I should hurry to prevent a killing because as a man of God it was my duty."

Rourke's brows lowered. He stared at the smaller dark man. He was about to ask a question, when the priest held up his hand. "In one moment, please. Let me finish. He said this man was hiding across the alley behind your saloon where there is an old fence. He was going by stealth to the north end of town to shoot a man in a buggy."

Jim let his breath out very slowly without taking his eyes off the priest as he said, "Father, you know who got shot, don't you?"

"Yes, companion . . . So here I am . . . It worried me. It frightened me. I know of hardship and bloodshed."

"What did you do, Father?"

"Well . . . nothing. That old man made me uncomfortable. He walked away before I could ask him how he knew these things. I should have gone after him, of course, but I didn't . . . I didn't come up here either . . . I have prayed to be guided. I can say to you only that I am haunted from back in my childhood. I am afraid of such things so I go at once and pray."

"Did you hear a gunshot, Father?"

"No. I was inside the mission. But I know there was one; the people in Mexican-town heard it; they talked and remained mostly inside."

"Father . . . Who was the man skulking behind the old fence?"

The priest spread both arms wide, palms up. "I don't know. As I told you, friend, when the old man walked away, I went to pray. From inside the mission it would not be possible to hear a gunshot. A cannon, yes, a gun, no."

Rourke got himself a jolt of whiskey and offered the bottle. The priest declined.

Rourke went to the cash drawer, filled one

hand with silver, went back, and offered the money to the priest, who shrank from accepting it until Jim said, "For the poor box, Father, not for what we have discussed."

As the priest reached out a hand, Rourke also said, "Father, between good friends many things are secrets. Don't worry."

After the priest left, Rourke went to a chair among the saloon's poker tables and sat gazing out into the dusky roadway, where there was almost no traffic, where stores had lights showing, where oncoming night was solidly settling.

He was still sitting there when old John Bacon, the town carpenter, walked in and blinked. "You run out of coal oil, Jim?"

Rourke went to light the lamps. The older man stood at the bar, gazing solemnly at Jim Rourke. "Well, I don't have a notion of what's goin' on except that usually when there's somethin', men meet in here. Only tonight everyone's actin' different. There's a light up at the firehouse, where the town council meets . . . Whiskey, Jim, an' just what in hell is goin' on?"

Rourke answered the question with one of his own as he set up the bottle and glass. "Did you make the box for Doc?"

"Yes. Slade told me they figure to bury

him tomorrow." The older man with work-roughened large hands downed his drink and pushed the glass forward for a refill. "Bad enough some murderin' son of a bitch killed Doc, but there's somethin' else wrong. Slade wouldn't talk about it. Him'n me been friends fifteen, sixteen years. My shop is next to his." The older man paused to watch the glass being refilled and reached for it as he grumbled on. "Couple of men come down to the shop, mutterin' about you maybe knew somethin' about Doc gettin' shot. I told them to get out of my shop, I'd known you too long to believe talk like that an' they'd ought to be careful because you got friends around town who won't like that kind of talk . . . Jim?"

Rourke replied to the quizzical look he was getting. "I don't know what's goin' on, but I'd give a pretty penny to find out. By any chance did you meet a sort of Mex-lookin' rangeman a few days back? He hung around town for a few days. Nice-actin' feller with sort of reddish brown eyes?"

The carpenter downed his second jolt and wagged his head. He hadn't done business for any rangemen in a long time. He had no reason to recall seeing any either, probably because they were always around, and in his line of work they meant no more to him than anything else that he had no particular interest in.

But he was curious. "Nope, not that I recall. What about him?"

"Well . . . Nothin' I guess, John, except that I'd like to talk to him."

"Is that part of what's goin' on, Jim?"

"It seems like it."

The carpenter had arrived at the saloon, because if anything was happening in town that would be the place to find things out. He departed feeling fine, but without having learned a damned thing. He had put in a long day making Doc's box, among other work, and as he left the saloon he felt just good enough to go home and bed down. When a man gets on the sundown side of seventy, there are times when the best part of a day is when it's over with. That's when a bed overtakes everything else in a man's mind. Especially after he's had a couple of snorts of popskull.

The following morning Rourke went down to the cafe for breakfast. He did it defiantly, expecting to meet other men down there who would act as though he did not exist.

It was partly true. Other diners slid glances in his direction, then concentrated on their food without making a sound. Usually the cafe had lively conversation over breakfast.

This morning Rourke could hear a man slurping coffee through a thick mustache from the opposite end of the counter, and the cafeman barely nodded as he brought breakfast. He and the cafeman had been friends for years. Today the cafeman was not outright hostile, but he was not friendly either.

Rourke was a good feeder, and he lit into his meal as though none of the other men were in the cafe. Several paid up and departed before Jim was half through. By the time he had swabbed up the last of the bacon fat with a piece of bread, the cafe was empty.

He called for a refill of java. When the cafeman came to comply he had his back to Jim, who leaned off the counter. When the cafeman turned with the refilled cup Rourke said, "I understand you was up at the firehall last night." It was a wild guess. "What did the council decide?"

The cafeman raised dark eyes as he replied, "Nothin' as usual. Enough hot air to fill a balloon."

"About me?"

"You was mentioned, Jim."

"They wanted to lynch me?"

The cafeman put his pot aside and leaned on the pie table as he crossed both arms and gazed at Rourke. "I won't say that didn't come up."

"What stopped 'em?"

The cafeman examined a hangnail with considerable concentration. "Slade an' that old screwt of a harness maker. Somethin' was damned wrong. They wouldn't say what it was, but this mornin' when I went to the mercantile for flour an' sugar the clerk told me about them findin' a hangrope in your trash barrel. He said Slade and Bedford an' Dugan was in the saloon with that rope. They said they found it in your trash barrel. The clerk said he'd sold that rope to a rangeman. It was the same rope hangin' in a tree down where Ed Ballinger was shot." The cafeman's gaze was stone-steady. "The store clerk said when you asked how that rope got in your barrel, Slade'n the others looked like kids caught with their hands in the cookie jar. I think they put that damned rope there. What do you think?"

"I think you're right. Only I'd mostly like to know where they got that rope."

The cafeman thought a moment, then nodded. "For a fact. If it's the same rope down where the marshal was killed, who took it down an' brought it back to town? That's worth askin' around about, ain't it?"

Rourke put coins beside his empty plate, winked at the cafeman, and walked out into a clear, cool, faintly flower-scented morning.

The man he left leaning on the pie table continued to lean there, gazing into the roadway where an old battered freight wagon was grinding ponderously southward through town behind a hitch of eight Mexican mules.

Rourke did not go directly back to the saloon. He crossed the road and was approaching the pole gates of the corralyard when a coach emerged with Walt Bellamy on the box. Walt either did not see Rourke or elected not to see him, although it was more likely the former than the latter; navigating past those two log gates without rubbing hubs required skill and concentration.

Jim waited until the rig was in the roadway then entered the yard, where a lithe young Mexican was coiling rope. He asked where Mister Bedford was. The Mexican smiled, shrugged, and continued to coil rope as he said, *"Yo no sé."*

Jim crossed back to the saloon, made coffee, and sat at a poker table. He would go find that old Mexican the priest had mentioned. It was not possible that anyone could have known the killer was sneaking behind that old fence unless the old man himself had been the skulker. He could not possibly have gotten back to Mex-town before the killing occurred.

What genuinely baffled the saloonman was that the priest had said the killing would occur when it did, according to that old *peon*. It sounded like one of those Mex-town myths which abounded. In New Mexico, there were always *fantasmas*.

He would have to speak to the priest again. It no longer worried him that he had come within an ace of getting lynched, and he thought he knew who had put the hangrope in the barrel, but what he was more curious about was how the man who put the rope there had got the thing.

He had a bushel basket full of questions for the priest, or someone anyway.

11

A Return to the Ruin

Martin Bedford took a long chance. This time he made no effort to contact *Des Molacho*.

The violent spring had passed. Summer was now over the land, which meant soaring temperatures. There were several things New Mexico was noted for. One was searingly hot summers once the full season arrived. Another was natural hostility; bushes had thorns, spindly trees gave no shade, water was never where it should be, crawling creatures had venom, the earth was mostly poor — and distances were usually great.

Before Martin Bedford reached the haunted old pueblo in its protected place, he was sweating enough to have soaked clothing. His mood was bad and desperate. But foremost, he had come out here on his own with no idea whether Halcón would be here.

Since the ordeal at Rourke's saloon the

night before, Martin would trust no one.

Bedford had decided that rather than pay Halcón six hundred dollars he would take care of the two men he thought were reasoning their way very close to Martin's secret, the killing of Henry Drake. He had managed to bushwhack Doc, but almost immediately things had gone bad, beginning with the rope. While sneaking down the alley before the shooting to put it in Rourke's trash barrel, he had almost been thwarted by barking dogs. He'd had to skulk behind an ancient fence to avoid detection.

He had convinced the blacksmith and the harness maker that Rourke was the most likely suspect for Ed Ballinger's murder, exactly as he had used sly innuendo to make it appear Rourke had been involved in Henry Drake's murder.

Folks were already wondering about Rourke for bringing that shovel back from the mission cemetery. By darkly hinting, it had been easy to convince folks Rourke engineered two murders and probably the most recent one.

Then that damned store clerk had walked in. Listening to the clerk, Martin's legs had become so unsteady he'd had to sit down. As the timid damned store clerk drove enough of a wedge into his effort to get Rourke lynched, he'd had an almost sick sensation not just of failure but of imminent personal danger.

He had a wad of money in his pocket as he crested the slight *barranca* above Anasazi Pueblo. If the hired killer was not down there, Bedford had no idea what he would do — probably run for it; he was very close to something he'd never experienced before: panic.

His dripping sweat was not altogether the result of a fiercely burning overhead sun as the horse began the descent into the wide place where the old ruin was located.

Halcón was there! Martin's heart briefly faltered; at the same time he felt enormous relief, he also had a feeling of distinct uneasiness.

The rangeman was leaning in the shade of an old wall, motionless and expressionless as he watched Martin leave the path and start toward him. The rangeman watched as Martin drew rein and ran a soggy cuff across his face. Halcón showed no perspiration at all; even though the shade in this place obscured direct sunlight, it did not mitigate heat.

The big bay horse was indifferently cropping feed near the spindly warm-water creek. He showed no interest in Martin's horse, nor the men, as Martin swung to the ground.

This time the stranger started the conversation. He half smiled as he said, "Well, it's good you came, but the price is still six hundred dollars."

Martin sighed and dropped both reins so his horse could seek grass. "You said three hundred each. Now there's only one — the saloonman."

Halcón barely nodded. "Six hundred dollars, Mister Bedford."

"But there's only one man."

"Yes, I know that, but your town is stirred up. People are talking and wondering. You didn't save money by trying it yourself. You made it more difficult for me. Six hundred dollars."

Martin stood gazing at the copper-hued man. "You knew about Doc?"

Halcón ignored the question. "Six hundred dollars. I will take care of the saloonman, but I would give you some advice. Even without one more killing, they are already working around to suspecting you. If you hand me six hundred dollars right now, my advice would be for you to get on that horse and go in any direction but toward Calabasas. And keep riding until you see snow."

Martin frowned. "In summertime?"

"Until you see snow. Yes, in summertime."

"I have things back there I can't just walk away from."

"They will lynch you, Mister Bedford. Believe me, you can count on what I tell you. If you ride back to Calabasas, they will hang you from the cross-member of your own corralyard."

Martin's legs were rubbery again. He sank to the ground. Halcón smiled downward. "To save a few hundred dollars you have ruined yourself. Give me six hundred and I'll take care of the saloonman. But that's all. After that I leave."

Martin fumbled in a pocket, withdrew a soggy wad of greenbacks, and held them out without looking up. Six hundred dollars. His throat was as dry as dust, but he made no move to arise and go to the creek.

Halcón pocketed the money and lingered. Always before, as soon as he had his pay he departed. This time he rolled a quirley with infinite care, lighted it, and trickled smoke as he gazed at the stage company's man.

He had a pleasant voice under all circumstances. Now, as he addressed Bedford, the tone was gentler than the words. "This has happened before, Mister Bedford. Let me explain something to you. Anyone who does what you did after asking me to do it for you has terrible things happen to them. You, at least, are alive, because you only did half of what I was supposed to do."

Martin finally looked up. "You're not makin' sense, do you know that?"

Halcón laughed. "Your horse is drinking with the bit in his mouth."

"Let him. What do I care?"

"That's how they get colic."

Martin showed something close to either exasperation or bafflement. "I'm not worried about the horse, Mister Halcón."

"You should be, Mister Bedford, if you expect him to carry you very far after you leave this place."

Martin got to his feet, walked to the edge of the creek, removed the bridle, draped it from the saddlehorn, and walked back. This time he remained standing as he addressed the rangeman.

"All right. You kill Jim Rourke an' I'll take your advice and leave the country. Only how will I know you took care of Rourke?"

"Do you hate him?"

Martin's venomous nature showed in his face as he replied, "I hate the son of a bitch, yes."

"Don't worry about it. Maybe someday you can come back, at least on the outskirts, and ask about the saloonman. They will tell you he was killed."

Martin knew he would have to be satisfied with that, but what was really deeply troubling him was abandoning everything, his money box, his personal things, not particularly his job at the stage company's yard — he'd been looking for work when he got that job, he could look elsewhere and again find work. It had been nothing but headaches since he'd arrived in Calabasas. But there was something else only he knew about and had been very careful to conceal from a nosy town.

The widow Danton, whose husband had worked himself to death creating a huge ranch four miles northwest of town. Martin had been secretly courting her for six months. She brought out things in him he'd had no idea he possessed. She had agreed they would be married in the autumn.

That tore at him like a wound as he stood in the shade with the rangeman, who finally dropped his smoke and stamped it out. *She* would worry when he did not return. She was the only person in the countryside who would worry.

Halcón spoke quietly. "Ride north until you see snow, Mister Bedford. That's the best advice I can give you." The lean, coppery man caught his horse, bitted it with his back to Martin, snugged up the cinch, swung over leather, and, as before, did not look back as he reined toward one of the little trails leading to the mesa above. He had a job to do; those who knew him had never known him not to keep his word.

Martin's horse watched the other animal go up the trail and softly nickered. The tall horse being ridden away did not so much as flick his ears to acknowledge that he had heard.

The heat seemed to increase as the afternoon wore along; it would continue to increase even after sunset, by which time every rock, every acre of land, every plant, would release heat it had stored throughout the day, making it impossible for coolness to arrive before the early morning, somewhere between two and three o'clock.

It was customary for saloonmen to provide pieces of peppermint with their beer to provide at least an illusion of drinking something cold. It was also the custom, invariably among the Mexicans and to an increasing extent among gringos, to go to bed inside massively thick mud walls that heat could not penetrate, sleep away the hottest part of the day, and arise after dark to have supper and perhaps sit outside to talk or visit, or to otherwise take advantage of diminishing heat.

It was certainly this custom that influenced the crop of newborns come springtime every year, again invariably in Mex-town and to a lesser degree in Gringo-town.

The oldest buildings had adobe walls as thick as three feet. Inside, temperatures varied only slightly, regardless of the season. That was unquestionably why saloons like Jim Rourke's place and the *cantina* in Mex-town had customers during afternoons before *siesta* time.

Jim's business was slow recovering, but it did recover. What probably aided that recovery was the matter of some local mysteries. One was the abrupt disappearance of Martin Bedford, whose yardmen knew only that one of the saddle animals was missing along with Martin's outfit.

This was a minor consideration in view of several other mysteries, but as days passed and Martin did not appear, this too became an excellent source for rumor and gossip.

What made it foremost in the category of gossip was the arrival in Calabasas of the Widow Danton who, despite her best efforts at being discreet, added to the mystery — and to community astonishment — for while the Widow Danton was sole owner of a huge, very profitable cow outfit, and was entirely presentable as a person, up until her inquiries no one had an inkling there was a romantic streak to Martin's character. Nor were those who knew Martin convinced the widow's anxiety and forlorn look were not badly misplaced, but no one mentioned anything like that to the sorrowing widow.

John Bacon, the town carpenter, rolled his eyes at Jim Rourke and dispensed one of his philosophical observations derived from more than seventy years. "There ain't no creature on earth who is a worse judge of men than women."

Rourke drew off a beer for the old man, set it in front of the carpenter, and smiled. "You sure of that, John?"

"I ought to be. I had three sisters. One married a drunk — handsome, mind you — but a dead drunk. Another one married a preacher; one of them traveling kind that sets up a tent in towns, preaches hellfire 'n' brimstone an' passes the hat. They about starved to death. An' my favorite of the lot — little Barbi — she run off with a traveling man who wore spats over his shoes an' one of them elegant little curly-brimmed derby hats an' a big diamond stickpin in his tie. He left her broke an' sick down in Texas to run off with another female."

"You got to be right, John," Rourke conceded. "Another beer?"

154

"No, thinkin' about them girls, all dead now — Give me whiskey."

As Rourke went after the bottle the old man watched him. When Rourke returned he said, "You ever been married, Jim?"

Rourke dodged the question. "Martin always was a horse's ass. Maybe Missus Danton will never know it, but she is very lucky."

Bacon dropped his jolt, shuddered, and agreed as he wiped his eyes. "That's no secret."

"I never liked him, John. But after him fixing things to get me lynched, I'd like just once to meet him again."

"You never will," the older man exclaimed. "Not after what folks figured out. But what I can't understand is why he'd try anything like that — you being known well over the territory. . . . Maybe he was even meaner than we thought. Maybe he just come to hate you so bad he'd try to get you hung."

Jim leaned on the bar without speaking, gazing past the tops of his spindle doors at the dancing waves of heat.

This very morning he had returned from Mex-town with information about something he had not mentioned to a soul and which completely baffled him — and he knew about Mexican superstitions, legends, and myths as well as anyone else. But this time he could not even imagine an explanation unless he wanted to believe what the little priest had told him, which he never would totally accept even though he had seen the evidence and would never forget that either.

He had been in New Mexico too long; had heard every story the Mexicans had to tell and which they clearly believed wholeheartedly. And which Jim Rourke, among many others, not only refused to believe, but scoffed at.

But one thing bothered Jim as much as it had bothered the priest, and while the priest had an explanation, Jim did not.

12

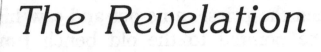

The Revelation

Father Cordero de la Cruz had been in the chapel when Rourke arrived in Mex-town. Two sweating grave diggers in the old cemetery shrugged and pointed toward the mission, said nothing, and went back to work. They had an earthen jug of watered red wine in the shade. Digging in this kind of heat required frequent periods of rest.

Jim hesitated. He was not a religious man, but having been born and raised a Catholic, he had inhibitions. He would sit on a bench on the tiled old ramada until the priest appeared.

He idly watched the grave diggers. They worked slowly but steadily, a good way to work when the heat was enough to wilt weeds.

Not a word passed between them, which intrigued Rourke; ordinarily Mexicans at labor spoke, chided one another, laughed, gossiped, told jokes.

Those two were silent, solemn, scarcely looking at one another as they worked.

Rourke became impatient. He went to the massive oaken door and rattled it. Nothing happened for a long while.

When the priest came out and saw his visitor, he pointed to the old bench Jim had been sitting on. As they sat, the priest spoke while watching the diggers.

"Did you know Arturo Valdez?"

Rourke shook his head. The name Arturo was common enough, as was the name Valdez. "I don't think so. What about him?"

The priest had a palm resting against the large cross draped from his neck down his front. He still did not look away from the grave diggers. "He arrived last spring, a toothless old man with his worldly goods on his back. He was always polite; he took over an abandoned old jacal. I visited him several times, which is my duty with newcomers. You understand?"

Jim nodded, guessed there was no way to hasten whatever the priest had to say, leaned his back against the mission wall, crossed his legs at the ankles and also watched the grave diggers.

"He is out there wrapped in an old blanket someone donated. He died." The priest shrugged slightly. "Maybe last night.

Maybe yesterday. He was known to his neighbors, but never visited, so neither did they."

Rourke asked a question. "He was old, Father?"

"Yes, very old."

Rourke also shrugged, it became inherent in gringos after many years in the Southwest among natives. In quiet Spanish he said, "It is the law of nature, isn't it? Old people die."

"*Seguro*. But let me tell you, friend — I am not a young man. I have seen many things. This I can tell you from my heart. There are more things we don't understand than we do understand."

Rourke fished for a cigar; his pocket was empty. He swore to himself and returned to watching the diggers. He knew as well as he knew his name this discussion was going to continue indefinitely. He had only come down here to ask again about the skulker in the alley; he hoped someone had seen the man and had recognized him. He needed the name; he was convinced it was the individual who had shot Doc Williams.

Father Cordero de la Cruz rambled on, his attention fixed on the diggers who were now in the shade with their earthen jug.

"So they came and told me. I went to the

159

old jacal. Friend, I tell you from the heart, it frightened me."

"What did?"

"He is out there behind some headstones, wrapped in the blanket. I went inside to ask guidance and to pray."

Rourke nodded. "For his soul."

The priest's reaction was so unexpected Jim was startled into sitting straight up. "*No! Never!* Get up and walk out there with me."

Rourke arose to follow the priest, eyeing him from behind with a puzzled frown. If he had stood inside the church and blasphemed at the top of his lungs he doubted that the priest would have acted any more shocked and horrified.

They passed the diggers with their jug, both of whom touched the brims of their hats and solemnly nodded as the priest passed. They neither smiled nor spoke.

Father Cordero de la Cruz walked gingerly to a flat-looking bundle wrapped in an old, threadbare blanket in the shade of a dowdy old tree. He stood for a long time, saying nothing.

Rourke stopped beside him, eyed the bundle, and said, "He wasn't very big, was he?"

There was no reply. The priest was now holding his crucifix tightly enough for his knuckles to look white.

Rourke frowned and looked sideways. The priest had both eyes closed, his lips moved, his free hand was holding to his robe.

Rourke saw movement; the diggers were leaning far around their tree, watching expressionlessly.

The priest softly said, "Open it, companion."

Rourke leaned, caught hold of an edge of the blanket, and pulled it back. For ten seconds he did not move. Beside him the priest was praying again, a barely audible sigh of sound in the surrounding hush.

Rourke closed the blanket and straightened up with a feeling he never afterward was able to define, except that it had been accompanied by abrupt coldness throughout his body.

The corpse was nearly flat. Old people often seemed to shrink into themselves, but this corpse was no thicker through than a man's forearm. And it was infinitely shriveled, with clawlike hands that showed every bone through dark skin as taut as a drumhead. The eyes were wide open; that was what held Jim Rourke perfectly still as he leaned. *The sockets had no eyeballs in them.*

He breathed deeply for a moment, looked in the direction of the old mission, and waited until the shock had passed before speaking.

He spoke Spanish to the priest. "He is like

161

a sheep that has been disemboweled, as though everything inside has been removed."

Father Cordero de la Cruz did not look down; he started back toward the shaded ramada. As he passed the diggers this time, they removed their hats.

Back on the bench in the shade the priest excused himself, disappeared inside the church, and came back with two glasses of blood-red wine. He had not spoken since they had returned, and he did not speak now. He crossed himself twice, sipped wine, and leaned against the wall.

Eventually he said, "I told them he could not be buried in the cemetery."

"Told who, Father?"

"The ones who came for the burial. It is the custom; respect the departed, pray at their grave. Do what can be done by the living in the face of what is unknown."

Rourke finished his wine and put the glass aside. "But the *grave* is inside the cemetery."

The priest barely inclined his head as he watched the diggers. "They saw only a poor old man who had died. They insisted, they were angry with me. So — later, when it can be done at night — I will take him up and bury him elsewhere." Now there was a trace of venom in the small dark man's voice. "In some canyon where the brush and

162

rocks are thick, where people will never go. You understand then, companion?"

"No," Rourke said truthfully. "But I never saw . . . Father, I have seen many dead men . . . but this one . . ."

The priest finished his wine, mopped sweat off his face, and faced his companion. "They will put up a headboard. It is always done, no?"

"Yes, I expect so."

"They will paint his name on it. Arturo Valdez. But friend, that was not his name."

"No?"

"No! It was Arturo *el demonio!*"

Jim sighed. These people and their damned superstitions. He leaned back and watched the diggers gingerly carrying the nearly flat bundle to the edge of the hole. They knelt down, let the shroud fall, and crossed themselves several times before arising from their knees to begin filling the hole. They had evidently seen the corpse, too.

The priest said, "Come inside with me, friend."

Rourke dutifully went. He had been inside the old church before. It was starkly plain except for the carved panels behind the altar.

Rourke crossed himself, did it again as the priest knelt, crucifix in both hands, eyes tightly closed as he prayed silently.

Rourke returned to the ramada and watched the diggers filling the grave.

He was shaken. He had been a practical man all his life, skeptical, at times cynical. It was not possible to operate a saloon and be otherwise. He had never believed in the legends, the mysteries, the tales that were a part of the life and faith of native New Mexicans.

Right now, watching the diggers finish mounding the grave, he groped for answers and found none. He felt again for the cigar that was not in his pocket, sank down on the bench, and leaned with both forearms on his legs gazing past the fresh grave to the spot where he had opened the blanket.

If he had lifted the corpse he was certain it would not have weighed five pounds.

Something that had been there in life was not there now.

He looked up when the priest came out to join him on the bench. "They wanted to carry him inside for a blessing at the altar," Father Cordero de la Cruz said.

Jim spoke his thoughts. "You refused. And how'd they take that, Father?"

"Inside the church they are humble. Of course they were outraged."

"Why didn't you just tell them the truth

— that he wasn't simply an old man, he was something evil?"

This time the priest delayed his answer, and when he replied he spoke slowly in the manner of someone who has had to wrestle with himself. "Pay attention, friend. I told them to be tranquil. I am a priest since before many of them were born. Last Rites and burial in sanctified earth where others who have deserved those things are buried would be sacrilege. I told them Arturo Valdez was already in the realm of his master before they found his body."

Rourke, who had completely forgotten his purpose in coming there, leaned back softly shaking his head. "A dream, Father? No one believes in demons. Maybe once but —"

The priest's interruption was given in a harsh tone. "Be patient with me, companion. Let me explain something to you. You have a saloon. I have never seen you in the mission church. You live in your own world, have no time for whatever else there might be. Friend, men like you are the exasperation of my life. Well, today with your own eyes, can you explain to me what you have seen?"

Rourke smiled ruefully as he shook his head. "No, *patrón.*"

The priest appeared to be somewhat mollified; he did not smile back, but he clearly loosened where he sat. For a time he held both hands clasped in his lap before speaking again, no longer with impatience or annoyance in his words. "There is something else, companion."

"I am listening, Father."

"Those like Arturo Valdez are . . . servants to those higher in hierarchy." The priest gazed steadily at his companion. "He was serving — someone else. Do you comprehend?"

"No."

"The one known as Arturo Valdez came here not alone."

"Otro demonios, Padre?"

"Yes. Valdez is now gone, no?" Rourke neither nodded nor spoke, so the priest continued. "His work is done, friend. Do you comprehend?"

"I guess so. What you are saying then is that there is another one?"

"Yes, but higher; someone much higher. He is still here, of course, unless all their work is finished here. If it is not — then the stronger one is still here."

Rourke raised his hat, scratched vigorously, and reset it. For the first time the priest seemed almost ready to laugh. "Gringo, whether you understand or not, at least you listen. Mostly gringos do not listen. They

166

know all there is to know, which is why they blunder so much. Companion . . . the reason I know the other one is still here is that if you had examined the shriveled corpse more closely you would have seen evidence of *capadura*. It is always done to a servant when his purpose is completed."

Rourke stared. "That shriveled up old man was castrated?"

"Yes."

Rourke was speechless. As with most people, incredulity, something totally unexpected and shocking, kept him silent for a long time before he said, "Let me ask, friend, where did you learn all this?"

The priest laughed and arose; clearly the visit was over. "It is a very long path to achieve a priesthood." For a moment the small dark man eyed Jim Rourke. "I will pray for you. Good-bye."

As he strode back to Gringo-town the saloonman was thoughtful. By the time he was back at his place of business he had reached only one conclusion. As long as he lived he would never, ever, mention what he had seen inside the old blanket, or what the priest had told him.

He was gazing out the door when a customer arrived, hesitantly. It was the town blacksmith, who only the night before had wanted to lynch Rourke. Jim nodded; the burly man nodded back. Jim drew off a beer and wordlessly set it before the blacksmith. When their eyes met, the other man mumbled and stumbled through an apology. Rourke knew Slade Downing well. The day he admitted he had been wrong would be the same day hell froze over.

Jim shrugged. "Forget it, Slade."

The blacksmith leaned and turned his beer glass. "John Bacon told me somethin' is goin' on he don't understand." Slade's eyes rose to Rourke's face. "After last night I got to say I think the same way. . . . Why did Martin disappear — just ride off'n and leave the corralyard without a boss, without so much as takin' his things out of the desk?"

Rourke leaned and smiled. "When you find the answer, Slade, *if* you do, I'd be obliged if you'd let me know."

"Yeah — an' everyone else in town." Downing tipped the glass, emptied it, pushed it aside, and wiped his mouth with the back of his thick, scarred hand. "We figured out how he done that trick with the hangrope. He put it in the trash barrel before we come down the alley with him. It had to be that. But, where did he get that rope?"

Rourke had been wondering about that, too, but after his visit to Mex-town the hangrope had just about lost its significance to him. He shook his head. "Maybe Martin could tell you. I sure can't."

The blacksmith snorted. "I feel sorry for that widow woman. It hit her pretty hard, him ridin' off and not comin' back."

Rourke nodded without heeding. He was back in Mex-town, looking at the corpse with brown skin stretched drumhead tight over its bones, with the fallen-in mouth and the sightless sockets above the mouth.

He shuddered. The blacksmith frowned. "You comin' down with somethin', Jim? There's summer complaint goin' around. You'd ought to get some sulfur an' molasses."

The blacksmith departed, walking straighter and feeling better now that he had confessed his mistake and had been forgiven for it.

But one of the accusers never again entered the saloon: the scrawny harness maker. In fact he avoided Rourke; even when they passed on the plankwalk, he would not meet Jim's gaze.

Some people harbored humiliation with the same bitterness they harbored hatred. They never apologized, even though they knew they had been wrong, and they never forgot.

Rourke's steadies began arriving as the sun

sank. He greeted them as he always had. If they noticed anything, it was the way Rourke would lean and stare into space between being hollered at for refills, but that could have been interpreted as the emotional aftermath of almost getting lynched. For a blessed fact, something like that would put its mark on a man.

The same questions arose as his customers mellowed-down their daylong, heat-scorched throats. The same answers were given, too. In time there would be variations. But one question eventually was asked more forcefully than the others: When was the damned town council going to hire another town marshal?

The way things stood now, authority obtained only when someone like the blacksmith or some other irate individual slammed the bartop and swore that unless a peace officer was found and hired, he would march up to the firehouse and hurl the councilmen out by hand.

Rourke was a councilman; he agreed with the need for a replacement lawman. Several customers had suggestions and recommendations, but as fast as one name was proposed, the other customers hooted it down for one reason or another. Near closing time Rourke made a suggestion that did not meet with immediate rejection but which would by the following day when heads had cleared.

His idea was to go among the cattle outfits, ask each cowman who his toughest, handiest man was, and see if there wasn't someone out yonder who could do the job.

After closing up, dousing the lamps, and dumping the last of the dirty little glasses in his washtub, Rourke went out back, sat on the step, watched a shooting star, and had a smoke.

Several things that had seemed vitally important earlier no longer did. For example, that skulker beyond the old wooden fence as sure as hell is hot had to have been Martin Bedford. Why he would shoot Doc was anyone's guess, but Jim would have wagered his saloon, including its liquid inventory, that the skulker he had seen had been Martin. Martin had been on Rourke's side of the main roadway, sneaking around in the alley so that he could put the incriminating hangrope in Jim's trash barrel.

And Martin had reached the north end of the alley just as Doc was returning to town in his buggy. But he could not imagine why Martin had shot the physician. As far as Jim knew, Doc had never been a man who made enemies.

Rourke tipped ash, stopped studying the

171

sky, and had a flash-back to the time Martin was in the saloon when Jim and Doc were speculating about murder.

Without a shred of clear evidence, Rourke plugged the stogie back between his teeth and swore. *That was it!* He and Doc had been fitting parts together, and Martin had stood there listening. Martin had been up to his damned ears in Henry's killing. He had loathed the storekeeper.

Rourke considered the end of his dead cigar, pitched the thing into the middle of the alleyway, went inside, and bedded down, both arms hooked beneath his head as he stared wide-eyed at the ceiling. *Demons,* for chris'sake? Demons that traveled in pairs?

But for a blessed fact, that shriveled corpse hadn't looked like he'd ever been a human being — or, if he had, it had been dozens, maybe hundreds, of years earlier.

He was going to get the priest to explain in detail that business of demons being castrated. That was the damnedest thing he'd ever heard. If anyone else had told him such a tale he would have walked away as he had done when Alex Jobey had spun that tale of Indians conjuring up ghosts and sworn he'd heard the devil laugh.

Rourke went to sleep a believer in what

172

he had seen with his own eyes; he shuddered at the recollection. As for the rest of it, hard-headed as he was when he closed his eyes this night, he thought, Who knows?

13

Making a Choice

Town councilmen were elected to office, and there was an established precedent for replacing council members who for one reason or another had not served their full two-year terms.

It happened fairly often. Slade Downing was appointed by majority vote to serve the balance of Henry Drake's term.

Jim Rourke would have preferred Walt Bellamy, but did not say so for one reason; Walt was fully occupied with his job as a whip for the stage company, and most likely he would miss half to two-thirds of the meetings.

At Slade's first meeting, he seemed to settle in well enough; he made no troublesome suggestions and was content to go along with the other members when a discussion required voting. But along toward the end of the session, when it was close to eight o'clock with a tad of daylight lingering, he started a sequence of events that brought the other councilmen up in their chairs.

"This business of a town marshal, gents
. . . There's got to be one. Everyone knows
that for a fact." Slade was sweating, probably
less because it was a warm night than because
blacksmiths just naturally sweated; it went
with the occupation.

"There's a feller I think might fill the job.
He's tough, rough, and they tell me he's a
fair hand with guns. I'd guess he don't know
much book law, but then, since I been in
the Calabasas country there's never been a
lawman who did. They knew right from
wrong, what folks should do an' what they
shouldn't do. It seems to me that's about all
a town marshal's got to know."

Jim and the others sat staring at Downing,
who was not known as someone who launched
into the kind of prolonged statements like
the one he had just concluded.

Jem Dugan said, "Who?"

Downing used a clean blue bandana to mop
perspiration off his forehead and farther up
where there was no hair.

"Jack Butts."

Not a word was spoken for several seconds.
They all knew the foreman of the Pothook
cow outfit, and the suggestion took them by
surprise. Jack Butts had been rangeboss for
Pothook for six or seven years. He was ca-

175

pable enough, no one questioned that; he was rough, hardheaded, fearless, and outspoken, but as far as any one of them knew, he had a lifetime job with Pothook. In fact, the last few years when Pothook trailed six or eight hundred head of beef to the desert country around Calabasas, Jack had ramrodded the entire affair; the owners had had enough confidence in him to stay at the home place up in southern Colorado.

Jack also decided when the feed was no longer good and organized the roundup and the long drive up north to cooler country where graze was still green.

A councilman who during working hours owned the gun works and who also did a little silversmithing raised his eyebrows in Rourke's direction. Jim shrugged. He would have bet new money Butts would laugh at the idea.

The gunsmith looked skeptical as he said, "Slade, why would Butts even think about the marshal's job? He's likely gettin' better pay where he is, an' he's doin' somethin' he must like or he wouldn't have stayed with it so long."

Slade relaxed a little. He had expected to be laughed at just for making the suggestion. "He brought in two bent wagon axles yestiddy. Some idiot thought he'd straddle a big rock with two work wagons . . . We set and talked. Them lads from out a ways always like to hear what's happenin' in town, specially since they already knew about Henry Drake an' Ed Ballinger. I said we had to find another marshal. He surprised me; he asked what the job paid. He set there a moment, lookin' at his boots, then he said, 'I'd like to try for the job, Slade.' I didn't ask him why, I didn't ask him anything. I just said I'd put his name before the council . . . an' that's what I done."

Rourke had a twinkle in his eye. After almost ten years he had just heard the blacksmith sounding as windy as a preacher.

The harness maker, careful to avoid meeting the saloonman's gaze, spoke next. "Well, we got to have one. Everyone knows that. As far as I know, Jack Butts might work out, only for the life of me I can't imagine why he'd want the job. Did you tell him about Doc being murdered right here in town?"

"Yep. Jack an' Doc was friends."

The harness maker considered his stained and broken fingernails. "Did you tell him the job don't pay much?"

"I already told you that," Slade replied, sounding annoyed. He scowled around the room. "Gents, it's gettin' late."

The grizzled, squinty-eyed owner of the tannery on the outskirts of town nodded in agreement. He had a wagonload of green hides due about sunrise tomorrow. Green hides spoiled fast in hot weather; a hide wagon was invariably followed by swarms of blue-tailed flies. He had to have his front gates open before sunrise. He slapped his legs as though to arise and said, "I know who he is, but that's all I know about the feller. We're not goin' to marry him, are we? If he can cut the mustard, fine — if he can't, we replace him, but we got to have a lawman."

Slade dropped another clanger on them. "By unanimous opinion, then, we agree to talk to him?" Without awaiting an answer he arose and went toward the door. "He's settin' outside."

Slade opened the door partway, jerked his head, and stood aside. The man who walked in and nodded was as dark as a Mexican from a lifetime out of doors. His eyes were faded blue, and he had gray at both temples, a bear-trap mouth and a square jaw. His clothing was weathered and faded, but the gun he wore offset the otherwise drab appearance. It had ivory grips, something few riders and not even very many rangebosses could afford.

Butts had a hard, practical smile as he went among the councilmen, shaking hands. He winked at Jim Rourke and took an empty chair near the saloonman. He demonstrated one thing right off. He didn't wait to be questioned. He said, "Gents, I expect you're wonderin' why I'd want a job that pays less'n the one I got. Well, I been trailin' down here and back up yonder long enough. I been winterfeedin' cattle in two feet of snow long enough. I'm plumb sick and tired of long cold winters, an' I've always liked the Calabasas country and the folks I've met in it. It's been in the back of my mind to make some changes for the last year or so."

When the lean, hard-looking man stopped speaking, his listeners looked at one another, except for the harness maker, who would not look directly at Jim Rourke.

Slade broke the hush. "Jack, what'll the folks you work for say?"

Butts gave an answer consistent with his character. "They can find another rangeboss the same as they found me when the one before me left the country. I'll send word for someone to come south to trail the cattle back up yonder when the graze is gone. That'll give 'em enough time."

Butts leaned forward, his expression intent, his pale eyes moving from one councilman to the others. "I've never been a lawman, but I'm real interested in who killed Doc an' the others. It don't seem to me a man's got to be a Pinkerton detective to find killers." He sat back and almost smiled at them. "If I can't do the job, you won't have to fire me. I'll know it before you do an' I'll quit."

Jim Rourke knew the rangeboss as well as did any of the others, perhaps a little better. The man's personality as it was now being projected was exactly the way the rangeboss thought and acted. Straightforward to the point of bluntness.

He eyed the other councilmen, but only the harness maker seemed annoyed at the stockman's take-charge attitude, but to give the devil his due, the wizened old man nodded, evidently willing to accept that a lawman should be frank and outspoken. But he had one more question. "You want to settle here?"

For the first time, the rangeboss seemed to hesitate momentarily before replying. He stated his answer as he looked directly and unwaveringly into the eyes of his questioner. "I told you I like it down here. I'll do the best job I know how to do, gents. I'll roust drunk riders on Saturday night or any other time they're troublesome. I'll do everything I can to find out who killed them townsmen. I never was real fond of Mister Drake at the store, but Ed Ballinger was a fair, decent man, and Doc Williams was a good friend. But my private life is no one's business but my own."

The harness maker got red in the face. Jem Dugan was by nature an acerbic individual. Rourke was watching him when Slade Downing spoke loudly. "You want him to wait outside while we take a vote?"

Rourke spoke for the first time since Jack Butts had entered the room. He looked directly at the harness maker, who still would not meet his gaze, as he said, "We can take the vote now. Slade?"

The blacksmith looked relieved. He had really been sweating through this. "Them in favor of hirin' Mister Butts — hands up."

Dugan hesitated, seemed to have a struggle with himself before raising his hand, but he raised it. So did the others.

Slade fished for his soggy bandana as he said, "That's it then, gents. Jack, when can you move your gatherings to the jail house?"

Butts arose. "Tomorrow afternoon." He looked at the others. "Thank you. You got my word, I'll do the job. Any advice you fellers want to give along the way, I'll be glad to hear."

Butts and the blacksmith exchanged a wink, after which the rangeboss departed. As the door closed behind him, the squinty-eyed tanner looked long at the blacksmith. "Why didn't you tell us he was waitin' outside?"

"I asked him if he wanted to set in an' listen to the discussion. He said it wouldn't be decent, that he'd wait outside."

Rourke leaned to arise, but the harness maker raised a hand. "One more thing we got to talk about before we adjourn."

The others gazed at the wizened old man and waited.

Dugan looked straight ahead at the wall behind Jim Rourke as he spoke. "I've heard complaints from folks, mostly near the north end of town —"

Rourke frowned. "Complaints about what?"

"The stink an' flies an' dogs dragging rotten meat into town from the tanyard."

No one spoke for a moment, then the tanner, who was also old and wizened, and who trailed the aroma of his occupation with him — which was less noticeable in winter than it was in summer — arose from his chair, squinted fiercely at the harness maker, and spoke caustically. "Just where do you think that leather comes from you make them sets of harness from? You got an idea that maybe the good lord makes hides off dead critters already tanned for your use?"

"I'm just sayin' what folks said," the other man snapped.

The tanner leaned a little and glared as he replied, "Well, you been talkin' to some gawdalmighty ignorant folks. Where do they think their shoes come from, their belts, their chair coverings, their damned — ?"

"I just told you, folks don't like the stink an' the flies. It's not anythin' personal. Folks just don't figure they ought to have to put up with . . . When the wind blows just right, I can smell them green hides all the way down to my shop."

The tanner turned and stamped out of the room. When he slammed the door the entire firehouse shook.

Downing waited a moment, then looked at Jim Rourke, who said, "All right, let's quit. I got customers waitin' an' a half-wit tendin' bar for me."

Dugan trouped outside with the others, managing at all times to keep at least one other person between himself and the saloon-man.

He knew where the others would go, and he knew what they would discuss over their beer and whiskey, and he was correct.

The saloon had a moderately mixed crowd when Jim walked in, followed by the other councilmen, less Dugan.

He paid off his stand-in, tied on his apron, and was reaching for his black cotton sleeve protectors when a large, beefy man said, "We was talkin' about not havin' any law. Jim, you'n these other gents was in council this evening, wasn't you?"

Slade Downing turned toward the beefy man. "We hired a marshal tonight. He starts work tomorrow afternoon."

Alex Jobey leaned from farther up the bar. "Where'd you find him, Slade?"

The blacksmith surprised Jim Rourke with his reply. Jim'd had no idea the blacksmith had humor in him. "Alex, we hired him off a chair at the firehouse."

For moments nothing more was said until a gravelly-voiced rancher turned toward the blacksmith. "Stranger? You gents searched around and brought in a — ?"

"We hired Jack Butts," exclaimed the blacksmith and turned to reach for the glass Rourke had set in front of him.

Rourke nodded to the men along the bar. "That's right. Jack Butts was hired on as town marshal no more'n an hour ago."

14

The New Town Marshal

The folks in town who knew Jack Butts at all only knew him casually from his trips to town and his infrequent visits to Rourke's place. His general affability was acknowledged, but there always was more to an individual than showed on the surface.

Butts took to law enforcement like a duck takes to water. Three days into the job he rousted two big freight outfits for using the main thoroughfare. He told them that hereafter they would have to go out and around town where they wouldn't crowd the main street and raise dust.

Folks nodded at their new town marshal, but a palpable reserve was evident. Those who had complained the loudest now said nothing and, without seeming to, avoided the new town marshal.

Jack demonstrated another trait folks in

town had no idea he possessed. He would lean on Rourke's bar and spin tall tales of his narrow escape from Indians some years ago, his fights with Mex marauders from below the border, his meetings with bears face to face, how he had one time shot a cougar off a man who was about to be killed. He'd also been in fights from Texas to Montana, sometimes with his ivory-gripped Colt, sometimes with his bare fists.

One afternoon Walt Bellamy passed the new marshal on the way into the saloon after having completed his run from down south. Rourke set up the beer as the whip beat off dust with his hat. Rourke placed a piece of peppermint beside the beer.

Bellamy finished the beer and leaned on the bar, sucking the peppermint. "You think Jack Butts'll take Ballinger's place?"

"No. No one can take Ed's place, but I'll tell you one thing, he enforces the law. He don't take any hard talk, not even from men he used to ride with."

Walt said, "If he can just find who killed Ed an' Doc . . ."

Rourke regarded the whip for a moment before saying, "It just about had to be Bedford who shot Doc."

Bellamy, whose work kept him going and coming almost constantly and probably had heard none of the local speculation, stared, then scowled.

Of all the outfits he had worked for over a period of about forty years, he had liked working for the Calabasas office of the Denver-owned stage company the least, and the reason was that he did not like Martin Bedford from the soles of his boots to the crown of his hat. Walt was therefore willing to believe what Rourke had told him, but he had a question. "Why? I know Martin was a good hater, along with being a clear-water son of a bitch, but why kill Doc?"

Rourke glanced past in the direction of the door. "You knew him better'n I did. He had a bad streak a yard wide."

"All right. But why Doc? As far as I know they was just barely noddin' acquaintances."

Rourke still avoided giving his real reason for thinking — *knowing* — that Bedford had killed Williams. "Why else would he ride off an' never come back?"

Bellamy had no answer.

After the whip departed, Jim Rourke had a few customers but not until evening would he have his regulars, so he had time to take a limp old newspaper to one of the poker tables, prop up his feet, and hold the paper in front of his face so reflected sunlight would make reading easier.

Alex Jobey came in, mopping sweat and whining about the heat. Jim put aside the paper, got the liveryman a glass of beer with a sliver of peppermint, and was ready to go back and read his paper when the liveryman said, "Marshal Butts's got a girl down in Mex-town. From what I seen she ain't no casual friend."

Rourke studied the liveryman, who was a raffish individual probably not to be believed; anyone who said they'd heard the devil laugh had pretty well shot themselves out of the saddle as far as credibility was concerned. Rourke said, "Did you see them?"

"Plain as day. I went to Mex-town to get some tequila from a feller I know. We went to his shed for the bottle, an' he beckoned me into shade on the far side of his shack and pointed while he was grinnin' like a tame monkey. They was settin' in shade out back of a jacal so close you couldn't have got a cigarette paper between them. She kissed him straight on the mouth an' the Mex with me almost strangled not to laugh. Butts pulled her to him — mind you, I seen this right outside her darned house. Jim, if folks been wonderin' why that rangeboss took a job here in town, I think I seen the answer. He's got a woman in Mex-town. Pretty, I got to say, an' the way they acted, take my word for

188

it, this wasn't the first time they ever met."

Rourke recalled Jack Butts's sharp answer to the harness maker's question. He had said in plain terms that he'd do his best as a town marshal but that his private life was no one's business.

Well, evidently Jack Butts had a private life. Rourke thought that, in fact, it *wasn't* anyone's damned business; on that point he and the town marshal were in perfect agreement. Nor was Jack Butts the first, and he sure as hell would not be the last to find solace down in Mex-town. It was an acknowledged fact that some of the women down there were prettier than a speckled bird.

But there was a point the town marshal seemed to have overlooked: in towns no larger than Calabasas, there was no such thing as a "private life," especially between the sexes. Maybe, in Jack's experience ramrodding cattle outfits, only appearing in towns for the mail and supplies, he did not realize how quickly people learned things about other people.

And, if Alex had told Jim, Rourke was completely satisfied he had told others too. If the town marshal thought he had a secret, by tomorrow night he wouldn't.

A few days later something happened that had folks upset. Jack Butts, evidently on information — Rourke never doubted the source — that someone had robbed a grave down at the old mission, went down there and during the course of asking questions had lit into a big Mexican and whipped him to a fare-thee-well.

Ed Ballinger had never done anything like that, and he'd been called to Mex-town innumerable times. Ed did more to promote good relations between the two parts of town than anyone ever had.

Rourke heard more of this incident as he, the blacksmith, Martin Bedford's newly arrived replacement, and half-deaf Pete Bradley from the pool hall were killing time during the hottest time of the day at Rourke's watering hole.

Amos Lawton came in looking distraught. The store clerk knew of the beating; everyone in town knew about it. What bothered him was the violation of a grave.

His listeners were equally interested in both instances, but as the store clerk ordered and guzzled down a beer, belched, wiped his mouth, then went on speaking, something else became clear to his listeners. The store clerk, like everyone, lived with daily violence that was as much a part of life as breathing, but grave robbing really horrified him.

Rourke kept his counsel. He could have

gone down to Mex-town wearing a blindfold and pointed to the culprit.

As for the fight, the big Mexican was a local *arriero,* whose pack mules regularly traded down into Mexico and back. He was, according to those who knew him, a good-natured man who had been goaded into a fight in the plaza with half of Mex-town looking on, and while he had put up a good fight, he was no match for Marshal Butts and was badly beaten.

It was decided by the men at the bar that Marshal Butts had chosen to demonstrate to Mex-town's inhabitants he was not to be trifled with.

They also agreed Jack Butts was turning out to be something no one had predicted. Slade Downing, who had sponsored Butts for the lawman's job, was chagrined and showed it when he said apologetically, "He's tough. We needed a lawman."

Amos Lawton stared at Downing. "Tough? He's a bully. I know his kind — they get worse and meaner. If we needed a lawman, why wasn't one hired who had experience at his trade?"

The clerk asked for a refill. As Rourke was drawing it off, Slade shook his head. "We needed one right now. Folks were gettin' cranky about the delay in findin' a replacement for Ed Ballinger. Jack looked good to me."

Pete Bradley had been having difficulty following the conversation, but by cupping a hand behind one ear he had managed to hear most of it. Now, he lowered his hand and frowned at Slade Downing. "All right, Jack looked good to you. An' he is good up to a point. But Slade, either that badge went to his head or he's got a mean streak you didn't know about. Whatever the reason — you got to get rid of him before he kills some drunk cowboy or does somethin' else folks won't approve of."

Downing's eyes widened. "Me? Hell, the whole council voted to hire him."

The pool-hall proprietor turned on Jim Rourke. "You're on the council," he said with clear meaning.

Rourke gave the only reply he could. "We can call a meetin' of the council and take a vote. That's how we hired him, that's how we got to fire him. Jack said if we didn't think he was doin' the job he'd quit, remember that, Slade?"

The blacksmith nodded dolefully. The new stage-company man stood up. "They told me up in Denver Calabasas was a sleepy little place. . . . Gents, I got work to do across the road."

With the departure of the newcomer, Pete Bradley growled for a jolt, which Rourke provided. Pete downed it, turned to put a sulfurous glare in the blacksmith's direction, and marched out of the saloon.

Jim felt sorry for Downing. He knew from experience how hard it was for Slade to admit he had been wrong. In order to make it a little easier for the blacksmith, Rourke thought aloud the mistake was the kind that anyone could have made, and for a blessed fact it was the kind of error in judgment he had made many times.

Whether Downing was placated or not, a new arrival in the saloon ended the discussion of Jack Butts. As Father Cordero de la Cruz nodded at both men, Downing muttered something and left.

The priest stood at the bar, eyeing Jim Rourke. He asked in Spanish if Jim had heard of how the new town marshal had beaten the *arriero*.

Jim nodded. "We have discussed it, Father."

"That's good," the priest replied. "Because there are some angry people in Mexican-town." The priest half smiled. "The association between my people and yours has been good for many years, hasn't it?"

Jim nodded. "I will tell you there are people

in Gringo-town who are not happy about what happened either."

"Then something will be done, companion?"

"Something will be done, Father. . . . About that opened grave?"

The priest leaned on the bar. "You know?"

Jim smiled. "You said he could not remain there."

"Well, only you and I know."

Rourke looked directly at the older, darker man. He told him in Spanish that if only he and Jim knew, then no one knew. He also asked what had been done with the body.

The priest spread his hand. "No one will find him. If he is ever found . . ." The priest shrugged.

Rourke smiled. "Some wine, Father?"

"Thank you, no." The priest hesitated as he was turning away. "It would be best if the new town marshal did not enter Mexican-town for awhile."

Rourke nodded, watched the holy man depart, and gazed a long time at the doors. He could close his eyes and still see that mummylike, dried-out corpse without eyes, with its toothless mouth fallen in, with skin pulled taut enough for old bones to show through.

He would see that apparition from time

to time as long as he lived.

It was slightly past midday, with dancing dust writhing under a malevolent sun, before several freighters walked in, dripping sweat. He got beer and peppermint for them, listened to their complaints about the heat, the washboard roads, and the cost of horse and mule shoes, which had gone up ten cents a foot. After they had paid and departed to seek a trough of water to duck their heads in, the town carpenter came in, sighed with relief to be where it was cool, and watched Rourke draw off his beer without speaking. As Jim placed the glass and peppermint before him, John Bacon said, "Did you hear the ruckus across the road?"

Rourke had heard nothing but wagons rattling past and men calling to one another. He shook his head.

The carpenter considered his beer before speaking again. "Jem Dugan seen someone over across the alley, slippin' along with a carbine. He got the new marshal. They scoured all around back there. The marshal got mad. He didn't see no one and didn't find no tracks that looked very fresh. He took the old screwt around front and give him hell for bein' an old woman, for seein' things. You know Jem, he got mad right back. They had a yellin' match. For a spell it seemed

195

the marshal was goin' to yank the slack out of Jem, but he turned and walked away."

Rourke considered the carpenter as he said, "Did he really see something?"

The other man heaved a big sigh before saying, "You know Jem. He's as ratty as a terrier. Shoots from the hip every time he opens his mouth. I'd guess he didn't see anythin', even though he yelled at the marshal that he seen that skulker plain as day. Anyway the marshal cussed him out good an' walked away."

Rourke was silent as the carpenter drained his glass, paid, nodded, and went back out into the fierce heat.

Rourke remained behind the bar, thinking back, but after a couple of days had passed, the menace in the priest's words seemed less vivid, certainly less convincing to someone who did not believe in such things as Father Cordero de la Cruz had mentioned.

He shook his head about the harness maker, too. Why would anyone be skulking out beyond the alley, carrying a carbine? Jem Dugan had always impressed Rourke as a nervous, waspish individual who, as the carpenter had said, shot from the hip, which meant he shot off his mouth without thinking.

15

The Priest's Explanation

Rourke was back at the same table with the same old newspaper when Ned Cooper, the new corralyard boss, came in. He commented on the diminishing heat on this particular day.

Rourke went to draw off a beer as he told the company man that when it cooled off after being very hot in the Calabasas country, there was usually rain.

The younger man — Cooper did not appear to be over thirty — drank, put the glass aside, and asked Rourke about Martin Bedford.

Jim's reply was careful. "I'd guess you've talked to your yardmen. Maybe others around town."

Cooper nodded. "So far I haven't found many folks who cared for him. But the way he left — just rode off — don't make sense to the people I've talked to."

197

Rourke's reply was cool. "It didn't make sense to me either, but then Martin an' I was never close friends."

Ned Cooper turned his glass in a sticky little pool. Rourke knew the sign: all his life he had seen people who had something to say trying to figure out a prudent way to say it. Jim polished several glasses while he waited. Eventually the newcomer to town raised his head.

"You knew Doc Williams?"

"As well as one man ever knows another man," Rourke replied, polishing a glass.

"I've only been here a few days . . ."

"But you've heard stories. When you're as old as I am you'll know the only way to keep a secret is to tell it first."

Ned Cooper smiled a little and drained his glass. As Rourke moved to refill it, Cooper shook his head. "I never was much of a drinker, Mister Rourke."

Jim's eyes twinkled. "I was never much of a Mister Rourke. Just plain Jim."

"I heard that Martin Bedford shot Doctor Williams, which is why he rode off and never came back."

Rourke was not exactly surprised; eventually someone was bound to come up with that notion. When he asked Ned Cooper who had said that, the stage company man accepted the refilled glass he hadn't asked for as he said, "A young Mexican at the yard."

Rourke knew the man; they were acquaintances, but that was all. He did not know the yardman's name.

While he was considering this, Ned Cooper volunteered something else. "He told me Mister Bedford left the yard a half hour early — wearing a gun, which the yardman said he almost never did. He said Mister Bedford and the doctor was in some kind of argument in your saloon before he was shot."

Rourke put aside his towel. That young Mexican had figured things out very well. But all Jim told Ned Cooper was that if he hung around town long enough he would hear ten other possibilities, then he changed the subject.

After Cooper departed, Jim Rourke resumed polishing glasses. How had the young Mexican known there had been an argument, which actually had simply been a difference of opinion, and not a very forceful one at that. His conclusion was shrewd: The young Mexican had been employed as a yardman before Martin Bedford arrived to run the station, and like everyone else who was even reasonably close to Bedford, he came to recognize his moods. The day he had returned from the saloon Bedford was in a foul mood, which of course his employee noticed.

What troubled Rourke was why Martin had been so upset. The discussion in his saloon hadn't gone beyond the point of speculation. The subject had been . . . Jim suddenly straightened up and put the polished glass aside.

He and Martin had talked about possibilities; Jim remembered telling Bedford it looked to him as though whoever had shot Henry had been waiting for him exactly as they had been lying in ambush for Ed Ballinger.

Martin had not said a word; he'd gotten pale in the face and had walked out of the saloon. Shortly after that, Doc had been shot to death and Martin had disappeared.

Rourke, who, after Martin's disappearance, had been sure who Doc's killer had been, now had a very strong hunch he knew who was behind the other two killings. Whatever Bedford's motive, and a man of his violent character did not have to be moved by very deep emotions, Rourke cared less about why he had got two men killed than about a powerful suspicion that he had.

He went back to polishing glasses until he had them lined up on the backbar; he stood a moment gazing at his face in the mirror. Slowly, very gradually, an idea came to him;

it was almost as though his reflection were telling him something. If Father Cordero de la Cruz was correct about there being two *fantasmas,* or whatever he called them, and one had been dismissed because he was no longer needed, then where was the other one?

The dark priest had gazed steadily at Rourke as he said these things; whether he was trying to caution Jim, the priest had not said, but his expression as Jim recalled it, had seemed to be suggesting a warning.

He threw his apron atop the bar, barred the roadway door from the inside, swore to himself all the way out into the alley, and would have denounced himself for a fool and worse except for one thing: the stark recollection of the frightening scarecrow of a man wrapped in an old blanket. *That* much was indisputable. The rest of it he could probably, given enough time, explain away by rational logic — but not the old mummy.

The priest was not at the mission, he was told in the doorway by a very handsome Mexican woman; he had gone to pray over a woman having a difficult childbirth.

Rourke, a man hardened by life, turned bright red at the handsome woman's candor. In Gringo-town a woman would simply have said the priest was not at the mission.

The handsome woman leaned in the doorway, regarding Jim with direct dark eyes. There was something about her . . . She said, "I recognized you when you came close. You have the saloon where the town marshal rests."

Rourke's eyes narrowed slightly. He addressed her in Spanish. "I do not know your name. I apologize for that."

She replied in English with a sardonic twinkle to her dark gaze. "Lola Bohorquez." After a slight pause she also said, "I'm the friend of the new town marshal."

Rourke nodded pleasantly. "For how long?" he asked.

"Two years. Maybe a little longer."

Well, that vindicated the old flannelmouth liveryman who had related how this beautiful woman and Jack Butts had acted toward each other. Now, if Alex Jobey would just admit that his story about hearing the devil laugh had been one of his tall tales . . .

"*Señor,* if it is important I can tell you which house to go to to find the priest."

As Rourke was about to reply he caught sight of the thick, short figure dressed in black with a large crucifix swinging as he approached. He pointed. The handsome woman leaned out the door, looking, and said, "I had better get back to work."

She closed the door, and Rourke sat down

on a bench. When he recognized his visitor sitting in the shade of the overhang the priest smiled and made a small salute with one hand before sitting on the same bench and looking inquiringly at the saloon man.

Rourke's tale was long and rambling. He spoke of everything he knew, which was not much, and all he suspected, which was much more. When he was finished, Father Cordero de la Cruz settled comfortably on the bench gazing past the shade to an open grave with mounded earth piled high on the side.

In his quiet, almost resigned way, the priest said, "Companion, I don't expect you to believe. I know that the last time we talked, you went back to Gringo-town with more doubts than certainties. Well, for you I will try once more. In the beginning —"

"No, Father, just explain about *them*. I saw the one you dug up. I want to know about the other one — if you are dead certain he exists." Rourke gazed at his scuffed boots. "That one you dug up —"

"The demon."

"All right, the demon. He was old, wasn't he?"

"Very old."

"Well — why castrate one so old?"

"Why? There is no certainty, but we have seen it many times over the centuries. We think it is to indicate to the demon that he has served his purpose, has done all he is supposed to do, and must then take his personal parts and return."

Rourke frowned at his boots. "Couldn't they just *tell* him?"

"We don't know, companion. All we know is the evidence of our eyes. Always, when their duty is finished, they are castrated."

"Maybe that's what he died of, Father. Shock."

"Companion, he was castrated after he was dead."

Silence settled between them. Some birds in a treetop beyond the open grave were squabbling over territorial rights; closer, some goats bleated.

The priest faced Rourke as he said, "What we must worry about is why the other one is still here."

"How do we know he is, Father?"

"Maybe he isn't, but believe what I tell you when I say they arrive in pairs, and each is found dead and castrated after they have done whatever they came to do . . . if they are found at all."

"Maybe the other one is gone, too. Maybe his shriveled body is hidden in some canyon. Maybe he was buried elsewhere."

"Companion, this one was a minor demon,

a helper. I think they must have lists of old graves from which they bring up demons to move into a dead person's body and, in this case, come to Calabasas. We know he is no longer required. We also know the one he served —"

"*¿El Diablo, Padre?*"

The priest flinched. His voice was stern when he spoke again. "Listen to me, friend. For the sake of your well-being, show no disrespect. Not 'the devil.' *Señor Satán.* Never sound demeaning. It is not healthy."

Rourke took the rebuke well. "*Señor Satán,* then. If he is here, why did he come?"

"*¿Qien sabe?* Who knows? What is certain is that when he arrives, bad things happen. My guess is that his demon searches out the person in need of *maleficia.*"

"In need of what?"

"Of help performing bad deeds, evil things. I think the demon may be brought to being by terribly evil thoughts by evil people. The way a magnet works. You do understand?"

Rourke understood. His difficulty was believing. He did not doubt for one moment the priest's sincerity and conviction, but his own experiences in life had never even remotely prepared him for any of this.

The priest spoke again. "Until someone finds a new grave or a body that has no eyes and has been castrated —"

"Where?" exclaimed Rourke exasperatedly as he waved a hand over hundreds of miles of countryside. "Father, there are endless leagues of land."

The priest replied quietly. "That is it, then, companion. If a grave is not found, we have to assume it is still here, that its work is as yet unfinished."

Rourke stood up, shoved his fists into his trouser pockets, and scowled. The priest looked up. "Be cautious, friend. Very cautious. This I will tell you from my own conviction. His work is not yet done."

Rourke went back to Gringo-town in a bad mood. When he opened the saloon there were loafers outside, waiting in the shade. All but one noticed Rourke's black expression and said nothing; Alex Jobey's lanky hostler called for a drink and in the same breath stated that Jim had lost considerable trade by keeping the saloon locked until past midday.

Jim gave the hostler a sulfurous look, and didn't say anything until he'd set up bottles and glasses along the bar. Then he replied, "Everybody takes time off now an' then."

His voice had an edge to it. The man next to the hostler nudged him with a bony elbow and scowled. The hostler did not say another word. He downed his drink and returned to the roadway, where he almost collided with his employer. Alex snarled at him. "How many damned times a day do you sneak up here?"

The hostler fled southward without answering. Alex watched him for a moment, then pushed past the spindle doors, got up to the bar, and said, "Jim, I'd take it kindly if you wouldn't serve my hired man until after quittin' time."

Rourke looked steadily at the liveryman, grunted something, and went to draw off another beer. He set it in front of Alex as he said, "Heard the devil laugh lately?"

Someone farther down the bar snickered. Alex's story had, naturally, spread through town.

Jack Butts arrived. He did not appear to be in very good humor, so nothing was said to roil him, not even after he growled about the damned saloon being closed. Jim got the marshal a bottle and glass, went up to the other end of the bar, and using a sour bar rag, mopped up spilled beer.

The marshal's mood improved after he'd downed a jolt. He looked up and down the bar, singled out one man, and said, "Did you see anythin' behind the harness shop when that old screwt an' I got out there? I saw you down the alley a ways, settin' a fence post."

The townsman shook his head. "Nothin' until you'n Jem come aroun' there an' got into an argument. Was there supposed to be someone else back there?"

"Yes — the old goat said he saw someone sneakin' along back there, carryin' a Winchester."

The townsman snorted. "I was there half an hour before you two come around. There wasn't no one carryin' a carbine."

Jack Butts saw Rourke's abandoned newspaper on a poker table, took his bottle and glass, went over there, cocked up his feet, thumbed his hat back, and ignored the others as he read.

One by one Rourke's customers drifted away, not because of the town marshal, although he had certainly dampened things by walking in, but rather because in another hour or so, it would be supper time.

16

Another Murder

The following day a meeting of the town council was convened at the firehouse. There were some minor matters to be discussed, and although Rourke expected the harness maker to take up where he had left off with his complaint about the tanyard, he did not mention it.

He might have been motivated to silence by the shaggy-headed old man sitting directly across from him regarding Jem Dugan with narrowed, threatening eyes as he gave off a tanyard aroma that prompted someone to open a window.

Slade Downing brought up the subject of Jack Butts, offering no solution and saying nothing as the others spoke. Slade was still chagrined about having advocated the hiring of Jack Butts.

Ned Cooper was there, too much of a newcomer to say much, but listening carefully to what others said.

Pete Bradley, speaking loudly, suggested contacting lawmen elsewhere for recommendations about hiring a new town marshal. There was no dissent, but Dugan wanted to know who should do this.

Pete suggested Jim Rourke for the job, and again no one dissented. Jim saw the new stage company man smiling slightly at him. He smiled back and rolled his eyes.

The next subject had to do with how to fire Jack Butts. Again Slade Downing took no part in the discussion, particularly when the waspish old harness maker thought someone should simply walk up to Butts and tell him it had been decided he was not the kind of lawman folks wanted.

This time, when Pete Bradley started to speak loudly, Rourke interrupted. "I won't do it. How about you, Pete? You brought this up."

The tanyard proprietor smiled and said if that had been put into motion, he would second it. Whether Bradley understood what had been said or not, he was looking at the harness maker as he spoke. "Jem, you'd be good at somethin' like that."

Dugan replied with a wolfish smile. "You already been suggested an' it was seconded. You get to take care of it."

Pete Bradley looked dumbfounded, but

only briefly, then his face colored as he nearly shouted, "I run a pool room. I never braced anyone like Jack Butts in my life. Besides I can't hear good; he might say somethin' I wouldn't hear."

No one said a word; they sat gazing at Bradley. He looked from one to the other and Rourke saw his shoulders sag as he said loudly that he would do it, but only providing someone good with weapons accompanied him.

No one volunteered. The council meeting ended shortly afterward with the issue of who was to fire the town marshal being the only piece of business that had been resolved.

Outside, with heat waves dancing, Slade strolled southward with Rourke. As they approached the saloon Slade said, "I been thinkin'. We need a real detective, not just an ordinary town marshal. Jim, don't any of us know how to go about findin' whoever killed Ed an' Henry. We need someone who can figure out a lot of things; someone who'll know how to run Martin down an' fetch him back for shootin' Doc."

Clearly the town blacksmith belonged to the majority who had accepted Martin Bedford's disappearance and the killing of Doctor Williams as proof that Martin had committed the murder.

Although Rourke was also convinced Martin had done it, he thought that now, after so much time had passed, no one would be able to find him. When he said this to the blacksmith, Slade neither agreed nor disagreed, he simply reiterated what he had said earlier: what Calabasas needed was a genuine detective.

They halted in front of the saloon, with Slade looking steadily at Rourke. Jim began to frown. "I don't have no idea how to get hold of a detective, Slade."

The blacksmith had a ready answer, and it seemed reasonable. "When you write them peace officers for Jack's replacement, it'd be easy to also ask about a detective, wouldn't it?"

Rourke sighed, nodded, and entered the saloon. His part-time helper removed his apron as Jim got close and spoke in a lowered voice. "He's been in for an hour."

Jim turned. Jack Butts was reading the newspaper again with his chair cocked back. He was holding the paper up to catch reflected light. All that was visible was from the waist down and a little of the crown of his hat.

As Rourke was looking in his direction Marshal Butts lowered the paper, met Rourke's stare, dropped the paper atop the table, and arose. As he strolled toward the roadway doors he said, "Time to make a round."

Rourke stopped him at the spindle doors. "Jack?"

Butts turned back. "Some trouble, Jim?"

"No. Folks are bothered by Martin's escape and —"

"Nothin' I can do about that. He's had too big a head start."

"What folks really want is for someone to be locked up for the other two murders. Henry Drake and Doc Williams."

The bronzed, lean man strolled back as far as the middle of the room before stopping to speak again. "Same thing, Jim. The trails are cold."

They gazed at one another with Butts waiting for more to be said, and Rourke becoming convinced that what Slade had said was true, Calabasas needed an experienced lawman, and this would be a good time to tell Butts of the council's decision to fire him, but he said nothing. Butts walked out of the saloon, and Rourke's helper said, "Mister Rourke, that feller scares the hell out of me."

Jim paid the man off, tied on the apron lying atop the bar, and drew off a beer for himself. There were no customers and wouldn't be for another hour or two. He went to the poker table abandoned by Jack Butts and picked up the newspaper. It was an old paper, probably left behind by a stage passenger passing through. Newspapers were rare in the Calabasas country. When folks got hold of one they read it from top to bottom and from right to left. Old news was better than no news.

Jim looked up as several men came in from out front. He recognized only one of them, a large, burly freighter with whiskers enough to hide nearly all his face except his eyes and nose. Jim had never heard him called anything but Frenchy, so he greeted him by that name as he put aside the paper and went behind the bar.

Frenchy introduced the other two freighters and asked for a bottle and three glasses, which Rourke set up; he hovered as the men downed their jolts.

Frenchy leaned on the bar, considered himself in the backbar mirror, stroked his dark beard, and said, "Jim, I been freightin' through Calabasas a long time an' this is the first time I heard so much talk about killings. We set up north of town an' met that old cuss who runs the tanyard. He told us no one's life is safe anymore in Calabasas. He said that after Ed Ballinger got killed everyone's been runnin' around like chickens with their heads off not knowin' who the killer is or what to do about him."

Rourke made a wide sweep with his bar cloth as he replied. "I guess that's about right. We hired a man to replace Ed, but he's never been a lawman before. He was in here a while ago; he told me the trails are too cold by now. Even the one where Doc Williams was shot at the north end of town not too long ago."

One of the other freighters spoke drily. "Sounds to me like you got a lawman who don't know his behind from a round rock."

Before Rourke could reply, Frenchy spoke again. "He told us about Martin Bedford too. He said he'd bet on his mother's grave Martin killed Doc Williams. He said Martin disappeared after the shootin', without even takin' his personal goods. . . . Jim, if Martin escaped a-horseback, someone, somewhere has seen him. A horse's got to be fed an' watered an' shod — an' rested."

Rourke had no answer to any of this except to pretty well agree with the freighter. Frenchy shook his head and reached to refill his jolt glass as he said, "Do you think Martin killed Ed an' the old crank who owned the mercantile, as well as Doc Williams?"

Rourke didn't explain the strange things connected with all those killings; he asked instead if the freighters knew a seasoned law-

215

man who might be interested in taking over in Calabasas.

The freighters gazed at Rourke in silence. They, like rangemen, did not cultivate lawmen. Frenchy counted out silver for the drinks, put the money atop the bar, and frowned slightly. "Sounds to me like you need the army, not a lawman."

After the freighters departed, a few regulars began drifting in. It was a little past mid-afternoon. The heat was still out there, but now too, there were shadows, thin ones that would lengthen as the sun sank lower.

As business increased and other topics were discussed along the bar, Rourke was certain that before long the main topic would come up. Too many murders with nothing being done was bound to rankle.

Marshal Butts arrived, ivory-stocked six-gun low on his right side, hat tipped down to protect his eyes from sunlight. He nodded around in a preoccupied manner, got a bottle and a jolt glass, and went over to the table near the roadway window to get comfortable and resume reading the newspaper.

Conversation dwindled for a few moments. When talk brisked up again the topics ranged from the heat to the poor likelihood of rain, the price of cattle, topics of interest to customers of a saloon in cattle country, but not the uppermost thought in many minds.

Rourke was relieved. He did not like dodging questions, which seemed to be all he'd been doing lately.

Slade and a grizzled old bandy-legged rancher from far out got into a mild argument over the best way to treat bent axles, common in rocky country. The old cowman was of the opinion that after being beaten straight, they should be dropped into cold oil for retempering. He said his father and grandfather both had always done that. Slade knew about oil-tempering, had tried it, but had never liked it.

He said the best way was to dunk the red-hot axle in cold water. The cowman was adamant. "Sure, that'll harden steel, but it'll also make it brittle. Now with oil, the temper ain't so good, but next time you bend an axle it'll warp. Cold-temperin' axles makes 'em brittle enough to break."

There were other discussions along the bar. From habit, Rourke heard without heeding. He was busy keeping glasses filled and bottles replaced.

Once or twice he glanced over to where Marshal Butts was tipped back in his chair with the newspaper. He seemed unaware of the men along the bar and didn't lower the paper to call for another bottle.

Jim went up the bar to where the liveryman was telling several listeners about a horse he had once traded for that could be ridden or driven in harness, a very gentle animal and a good keeper who would do whatever folks asked of him until he got tired of it, then would fold all four legs under him like a dog and no amount of thumping would make him get up.

The introduction of that kind of story among men who had owned all kinds of horses during their lives invariably prompted other recollections. After a while the laughter from that end of the bar and the tall tales drew other men from farther down the bar who also had stories to tell.

It got noisy. Rourke lingered up there only long enough to be sure the storytellers did not go dry, otherwise he washed glasses, swiped off the bar, and occasionally glanced at the poker table where Marshal Butts was reading.

He did not hear the shot. None of them in the saloon heard it. In fact no one knew there had been a gunshot until one of the men at the upper end of the bar stepped clear of his companions to expectorate in the direction of the nearest cuspidor, of which Rourke kept at least seven scattered around in strategic places.

The tobacco chewer who stepped back, squawked loudly, and stared in the direction of the marshal's table.

The marshal's hat was on the floor; Butts was folded over from the waist, face down on the newspaper atop the poker table.

Rourke saw the dripping blood; it puddled beneath the table. Like the others, he was stunned into immobility.

Slade Downing pushed past the other men and walked very slowly and deliberately down to the table, leaned over to grasp the lawman's shoulder, and almost immediately let go.

Rourke came from behind the bar, moving fast. He stopped beside the blacksmith as Slade half whispered, "Shot dead. Look there; hit from back to front smack-dab in the middle of the back."

Other men came over to the table. It was quiet enough to hear a distant dog barking. Every man there had seen death, several of them had seen death from gunshots, but they had heard nothing and had no reason to expect anything like this. The hardest among them had been so taken by surprise they stood at the table looking at the dead man in total shock.

Slade moved slowly to the window, saw the hole, and leaned aside to follow the probable trajectory of the bullet. He turned. "Jim, come over here."

They all came. Slade put his thick finger beneath the hole. One man looked and sounded awed as he said, "I never seen a bullet go through a window without bustin' the glass before."

No one heeded him. The old cowman swore softly, then gestured with both arms. "Get your horses. Some of you go across the road where that slug come from. Search every blessed building. You other fellers get astride. If the son of a bitch runs for it, as long as daylight holds we ought to be able to see him. *Move,* gawddammit, *move!*"

Rourke paused long enough to shed his apron and lock up from the roadway before following other townsmen who did not own horses in the direction of Jobey's barn.

Alex was napping in the harness room. His hostler heard men shouting, looked up the road, saw the mob coming, and scuttled back to vigorously shake his employer.

Alex awakened in a foul mood and swore at his hired hand as he sat up and reached for his hat. As the noise out front got louder, the hostler craned his head out the door and said, "It's Mister Downing an' — hell — half the town! They're comin' in here."

Alex sprang up, grimaced from the sudden movement, and went into his runway in time to see the men coming toward him, calling for saddle stock.

Alex hesitated until Rourke yelled an explanation, then the liveryman and his hostler moved swiftly. The store clerk was among them, and he thought of something the others had overlooked in their agitation. "You fellers better get guns."

That provided Alex Jobey with a little more time. As the men fanned out for home and their weapons, the liveryman and his helper worked fast. Not fast enough, according to some of the impatient townsmen, but as fast as they could.

As the first men were returning with weapons the old cowman flashed past with several other mounted riders and yelled, "What'n hell you boys waitin' for?"

By the time everyone was mounted, the old man and his riders had turned westward and were riding diagonally upcountry from the lower end of town.

Rourke wondered about their course, but Slade didn't; he put his livery animal into a lope and followed the cowman.

Riders were scattered; some of the livery animals were not very fast and some of the riders hadn't been astride in years and began to feel the pounding almost before they got clear of town.

Rourke and Slade caught up with the old cowman, who gestured northwesterly. "That's how he went."

Slade scowled. "How d'you know? We could be ridin' in the wrong —"

"Because, gawddammit, Jem Dugan at the leather works saw him. He didn't tell anyone right off because they busted into his shop, pryin' into every closet, nook an' cranny, and Jem was so mad he was jumpin' up an' down. He finally got hold of himself. He said he heard the shot, it came from somewhere in the alley behind his shop. He said he tried to tell Jack Butts there was someone skulkin' around back there, but Jack wouldn't believe him." The old cowman paused when one of his riders yelled and waved his hat. Rourke looked but saw nothing.

The old man booted his mount after his riders, leaving the townsmen to come along as best they could. Rourke still had seen nothing. The reason for the rangemen's excitement had not been a sighting, it had been fresh shod-horse tracks.

Half an hour into the pursuit the livery animals began to drag, so they continued at a walk, wishing for ranch horses that would have been able to catch up with the rangemen.

The townsmen did not see any tracks except those of the rangemen up ahead, but such was their faith in the experience of the old cowman and his companions that they never questioned the direction they were taking.

The heat was still fierce despite a slanting-away yellow disc. This bothered animals more than men; sweat from horses came from at least three times as much exposed hide as men had, so they suffered first.

The cattlemen stopped up ahead with a mile or so between where they had halted and the oncoming townsmen. When Rourke got up there, the craggy old cowman was rolling a smoke. He spoke to Rourke and his companions without looking up from his occupation. He inhaled, spit, and said, "I'd give fifty sound horses for the animal that feller's riding."

He pointed. "See them tracks? Well, there's no drag marks, an' the stride's as long now as it was when we first picked up the sign."

Slade had been staring from the saddle. He swung to the ground, knelt, studied the imprints for a few moments, then very gently traced their outline with a thick forefinger.

Without looking up or raising his voice he murmured as though talking to himself, "I haven't seen shoes like these since I was a button. Iron. Iron horseshoes." He twisted to look up. "Not steel like the shoes on your animals. Iron shoes." Slade pushed up to his feet, staring at the imprints. "First ones I've seen in fifty years."

17

The Pursuit

What they all feared might happen did happen, but not until they had been on the trail almost three hours; daylight began to fade. Summertime dusk would be along. However, this time of year dusk lingered awhile before night settled.

The old cowman, as wiry as a fried monkey, never let up. He muttered to himself about the townsmen being unable to keep up, but his riders were too interested in tracking to pay attention to laggards.

When dusk finally arrived, they stopped at a creek to tank up the animals, and while dismounted the old cowman came over to where Slade and Rourke were standing and wagged his head. "I'm seventy-seven years old an' I been around livestock — horses, I mean — most of them years. I never seen a horse, or even heard of one, that could do what the bushwhacker's horse can do. He ain't broke stride once, and there ain't no scuff marks in back to show he's tired. He just keeps goin'. Gents, if we catch this feller I don't care about him, but I want to see that horse."

They rode until it was difficult to discern the tracks, after which time two of the men dismounted to walk ahead and read tracks.

But the cowman was no longer hopeful. "By rights we should have at least caught a sighting. Come dark we can still track him by stoppin' often to lean down and see his sign. But when we start doin' that he's going to put more'n more miles between us . . . I'd give five hunnert dollars for his horse."

The rancher was correct. They were still tracking after dusk turned to night. The moon was a thin sliver and starlight was puny as they stopped near a bosque of trees to palaver. The old man said they could track him all night, which would only succeed in tiring them and wearing down the horses — and the bushwhacker would be even farther away come daylight.

"I hate to say it," he told them all, "but that feller's goin' to get away as sure as I'm standin' here."

The men muttered among themselves. The townsmen were willing to turn back. Even the ones who had ridden recently were sore, and all of them were hungry. The old stockman mounted and leaned on the horn, eyeing the townsmen. "You boys suit yourselves. I'd like to stay on his trail — I'd give a lot to lynch the son of a bitch, but . . . well, there's times a man wins an' times when he don't."

The old man led the exodus back to Calabasas. The townsmen watched, then fell to muttering among themselves again. Finally, they told Rourke they would go back. Several said they had never liked the town marshal anyway, and they sure as hell hadn't liked him well enough to ride their butts raw.

They seemed to expect Rourke to agree, but he stood beside his horse, making no move to mount. Nearby, the blacksmith watched Rourke.

When all but two men were mounted, someone asked if Rourke and Downing weren't going back with them. Jim looked at Slade as he said, "Go on." The blacksmith asked if Rourke was going back. When Rourke shook his head, the blacksmith looked at the townsmen and also shook his head.

When they were alone, the saloonman considered the sky, the foreshortened horizon, and the shod-horse imprints before he spoke.

"You got a business to run, Slade."

"So have you. They'll miss the saloon not bein' open a lot more'n they'll miss the smithy bein' closed."

Jim gazed at the other man. "Why? You didn't like Butts."

The blacksmith pulled a stalk of grass and chewed on it as he replied, "I never liked Martin, neither, an' Henry Drake wasn't friendly . . . I just don't believe in shootin' folks in the back."

They walked side by side, leading their horses as they followed the tracks. They had covered about two miles when the blacksmith said, "I expect the reason folks quit usin' iron shoes was because the newfangled steel shoes could be warped to fit, most of the time without using a forge. They was cheaper too. Easier to handle. When you bought a keg of them iron shoes, it took two men to lift it."

The moon slanted away; an occasional rodent-hunting owl passed. There were coyotes sounding somewhere off to their left.

Jim Rourke seemed to concentrate on the tracks, but in any case when a conversation was inaugurated, it was invariably the blacksmith who started it. Jim Rourke hiked along, head down, as though he was concentrating his full attention on tracks.

Neither of the manhunters were accustomed to walking considerable distances, so with chilly dawn beginning to show and they saw smoke rising from a log house about a mile or so dead ahead, they decided to stop there to, hopefully, get fed, and to rest tired bodies and feet.

They rode the last half mile, entered a tree-shaded yard where everything looked old, tied up their horses at the rack in front of the house, and were surprised when an old man, shaggy as a bear, called to them from the far corner of the house. They did not see the man, just the hexagonal barrel of an old buffalo rifle pointing at them. That caliber weapon shot a slug close to the size of a man's thumb, the first joint anyway.

Slade told the old man who they were and what they were doing out there. The old man listened, but did nothing for such a long time Jim Rourke thought he might not walk out where they could see him.

"You say you're from Calabasas," the hidden man exclaimed. Jim answered that Slade was town blacksmith and he operated the saloon in town.

"An' you figure you're goin' to run someone down? Two town fellers?"

Slade reddened slightly. Rourke humored the unseen rifleman with the slightly quavery voice. "We're sure goin' to try, mister. He shot the town marshal in the back, killed him. The marshal was readin' a paper in my saloon when it happened. Mister, what we'd like from you is — did you see a horseman go by here last night, or maybe —"

"Feller named Halcón ridin' a big thoroughbred-lookin' horse?"

Rourke replied dryly. "That's him, friend."

The big-bored old weapon disappeared, and moments later the man holding it stepped in sight. He studied the men in front and said softly, "You'll never find him. He's better mounted than anyone I ever saw. Them animals you lads rode into the yard . . ." The old man shook his head.

Slade and Jim were staring. The man may at one time have been taller than he now was. He was old, very old, but his pale eyes were keen and alert. His entire face was covered by a gray beard, the only color was around his mouth where the hair was light yellow. His clothing was clearly homemade from skins. As he leaned on the old rifle, gazing as steadily at them as they were at him, he spoke again. "Yep. He stopped here last night. I took a lantern out with him while he cared for his horse. Boys, I've owned more horses than you can count, but I never owned — never even *seen* one like that one. Sixteen hands tall if it was an inch, good head, good eyes, not young but not old neither. Had a chest on him like a barrel, legs with more muscle in the right places than any other two horses."

Rourke interrupted; he thought the old man's enthusiasm was going to continue until the sun was high. "What time of night did he get here?"

"I never kept time by hours. My watch quit runnin' sixty years ago. I'd guess maybe close to midnight."

"You put him up?"

"Well, I offered to. He was a real decent feller, smiled a lot, talked sort of soft . . . I fed him some 'possum stew and herb tea. He wouldn't drink any of my liquor. I don't care much for it myself, but a man makes things out of what's at hand." The old man smiled broadly as he continued his study of Downing and Rourke. "You'd do well to just give up an' ride back. You'll never catch him. . . . Murdered your town marshal? Well, I'm as good a judge of men as anyone else, an' I can tell you if he shot someone they must've had it coming."

Jim leaned on the old tie-rack, crossed glances once with Slade, and asked if the old man would let them pay him for something to eat. The old man shrugged. " 'Possum stew. It's all I got. Cooked up a mess first of the week, but I heat it every day so's it won't sour on me. Come on inside."

They exchanged another look before following the old man into his log house, which consisted of one big room badly in need of airing out. The walls were hung with an assortment of items ranging from bear traps to hides as stiff as wood. The stove was ancient and made of cast iron. There was a rickety table with three chairs. As Slade and Jim sat down, the old man pointed to his kindling box. "Had another chair but it give out a while back. I'll heat some of the herb tea — that'll hold you until I fire up the stove. . . . Saloonman, did you say? Before In'ians run off my horses I used to ride over that way for flour and such. But it's been thirty years now since I even got close enough to see the roofs."

Rourke guided the conversation around again to the man they were hunting. The old man made a cackling laugh. "Never in your life on them horses will you even see his dust. Believe me, lads, as long as he's got that big bay under him, if he don't want to get caught, no one's goin' to catch him."

They ate the stew, drank some of the herb tea, which was as bitter as original sin, gave the old man some silver, and left his yard with the sun climbing.

They picked up the tracks and paralleled them without stopping until late afternoon when their animals were beginning to tire.

This time there was no cabin, but there was a cold-water creek brawling past a bosque of white oaks in the middle of nowhere. Neither of them had ever been so far in this direction.

The horses rolled, drank at the creek, then remained along the soft bank where the only green feed was located. They cropped grass like there was no tomorrow.

There were trout in the creek, but they had nothing to catch them with. They made beds of skunk cabbage, which was excellent for that purpose if one didn't mind the smell, and talked until moonrise.

Slade Downing was a dogged man; had always been that way. He had never turned his back on whatever he was doing until it was finished, but as the moon soared and he reflected upon the undeniable hardships ahead, he wavered. He even thought out loud that unless Rourke was dead set on pursuit, he thought it might be as well to give up and go back to town.

Rourke's reply did not particularly surprise Downing; he had known the saloonman a long time. Rourke's reply was blunt. "We can wear him down. As long as we got his tracks we can find him."

The blacksmith closed his eyes. He was dog-tired, so sleep came quickly. The following morning when they were following the tracks again, the blacksmith was quiet. He did not believe there was any justification for murder any more than did anyone else, including Jim Rourke, but the farther they rode, following tracks good enough to see without difficulty even when they passed through stands of pines, the more he felt that as good as those tracks were, the rider of the big bay horse was mocking them, was deliberately making it easy for them to follow him.

By late afternoon, with a light wind blowing from the direction of some brushy foothills with forested uplands behind them, Slade waited until Rourke halted near another little creek, this one more placid than the previous one where they had halted. He got stiffly down, and while Rourke was removing his saddle, Slade said, "Jim, he could be over into the next territory an' still be goin'. We're ridin' ourselves raw. I think that old gaffer back at the log house was right. We're not goin' to find him."

"We *are* goin' to find him," Rourke growled.

His tone made the blacksmith look up. For a long moment he watched his companion. Jim Rourke seemed different; it was nothing Downing could define, but it was there —

a difference that was grim. "Tell me something," Slade said quietly. "You didn't like Jack Butts, so why are you so dead set on running down his killer?"

Rourke had his back to Downing when he answered. "It's personal, Slade. I want this son of a bitch real bad."

"Because you figure he killed Henry an' Ed?"

"Maybe. It's somethin' I can't explain. If I tried you'd think I was crazy."

Downing watched the horses cropping grass for a moment before saying dryly, "You keep this up, partner, an' I'm goin' to think that anyway."

Rourke turned. "Go back, Slade. Your heart's not in this. Mine is. If I got to follow him to hell I'm goin' to do it."

The blacksmith leaned and watched water run past in the little creek for a while before arising to go stand near his horse. "Jim, we been friends a long time. We've had our ups an' downs, and right now we're out here together. You can tell me what's makin' you act like this."

Rourke's reply was the same. "You wouldn't believe it. Go on back, Slade. When I catch up to him —"

"*If* you catch up to him."

"He's out there, partner. I'll find him

sooner or later."

Slade gave up. This conversation could go on indefinitely, and while they argued the killer was widening the distance between them even more.

When Rourke splashed across the creek, the blacksmith was behind him.

The day was late before they saw buildings. It was a large cow outfit; there were outbuildings, a big network of working corrals, big old trees around the yard, and dogs.

By the time they were approaching the yard, men were watching them. One man in particular, big enough to eat hay, was in the middle of the yard, wide-legged and scowling. Other men, riders from their appearance, were among the outbuildings, and while it was not normal for working rangemen to wear sidearms, every man in that yard had a shellbelt and holstered Colt showing.

Downing made a remark from the side of his mouth as they passed the first large trees. "They don't look friendly."

Rourke said nothing. He rode directly toward the big man standing wide-legged, halted, and nodded. "My name is Jim Rourke, I own the saloon in Calabasas. This here is Slade Downing, the town blacksmith."

The big man had a hard set to his face when he said, "What do you want?"

It was more than a blunt question, it was a challenge. It also held the mounted men momentarily silent. It was considered rude to act the way this man was acting.

Rourke replied coldly, "We want to know if you or your riders have seen a feller riding a big, thoroughbred-looking bay horse in the last twenty-four hours."

"Why? Is he a friend of yours?"

"Mister, he shot our town marshal in the back."

The men around the yard neither moved nor spoke, but the big wide-legged man did. He eased up a little. "In the back?"

"Yes, sir, in the back. The marshal was settin' in my saloon, readin' a paper. This feller shot him through the window — in the back."

The stranger's attitude changed. "I'm Hobart Booth. These lads are my riders. Yes, we saw this feller. Sort of coppery-hided like maybe he's half-Indian. He passed through last night. I was abed but I heard the shootin' and jumped up. He was gone before I got my boots and britches on. His tracks was plain as day . . . He'd shot three of our dogs. One, two, three, just like that. I think he figured to stop in the yard, but when the dogs run at him he shot them."

Slade said quietly, "It was pretty dark last night, Mister Booth."

The large man put his attention on Downing when he replied. "We figured on that, blacksmith. Whoever he is, he's a damned good pistol shot. Every dog was hit through the head — in the dark."

Rourke asked what time last night this had happened. The large man turned and repeated the question to a lanky, lean man leaning in the doorway of a shoeing shed. The lanky man answered curtly, "Maybe one, two o'clock this morning."

The large man faced Rourke and Downing again. "I got two good trackers on his trail. When they see him they're comin' back so's the rest of us can overtake him."

Rourke spoke again in that quiet way. "Mister Booth, your chances of findin' him are about as good as catchin' a ghost."

The large man's retort was short. "You think so, do you? Mister, this far from anywhere we been catchin' 'em for years an' leavin' 'em hanging from trees."

Rourke had glanced in the direction of the corrals. He asked if Mister Booth could spare two fresh horses, mentioning the condition of the horses he and the blacksmith were riding.

238

The large man had already appraised the animals as Slade and Jim were entering his yard. "I expect I can. For a fact those two you got look pretty well worn down."

He turned and called to the lanky man again. "Bring 'em two mounts, Jared."

As the lanky man moved to obey he threw an observation to his employer. "If Sam an' Wes can't find him, Bart, it don't seem to me a blacksmith an' a saloonman can."

Rourke ignored that to ask if they could get something to eat while they were waiting. The large man nodded. As they were walking toward the cookhouse Bart Booth added to what he had already said. His foreman, the lanky man he had called Jared, had got outside when the dogs first started barking; lately the ranch had been bothered by prowling cougars.

Jared was on the bunkhouse porch with his boots on when he saw the big horse enter the yard. He saw its rider briefly by the flame of his muzzleblasts.

He had told his employer he was too stunned at what happened with the dogs to move; he was standing out there in just his longjohns and boots with no weapon as the rider turned his big horse and left the yard in a lope.

Rourke said nothing. He distinctly remembered the pleasant stranger with the half-Indian look at his bar. He had not known his name, though, until that old hairy-faced hermit had mentioned it . . . Halcón. In Spanish, that meant falcon. A killer bird of prey.

18

The First Sign

When they were back on the trail, Slade dozed off and on in the saddle. Neither of them had much to say. More than ever Rourke felt that the man they were seeking was deliberately leaving a trail for them to follow.

When heat came, they watered at a creek and sat awhile in creek-willow shade. The inevitable happened; the human carcass can absorb a lot of punishment but it has limits. They both fell asleep.

Not until one of the horses, startled by cougar scent, snorted loudly in fear and stamped the ground, did they awaken. It was close to noon with a burning sun directly overhead.

They went to calm the horses, then took down their carbines and scouted for the cat, who was, of course, long gone.

They returned to the creek, splashed water in their faces, got astride, and continued their tracking.

241

Downing was very near the end of his trail when Rourke reined up and pointed. The tracks they had been following for two days had never deviated from a westerly course. Where Rourke was pointing, the tracks now bent around northward.

They followed for about a mile and got another surprise. The tracks were now heading straight east. Slade, who had been on the verge of quitting for the last few hours, made a silent observation: he had intended to abandon his companion and head back for town. Now, with the tracks going in that direction, he simply nodded his head when Jim Rourke said, "Well, I'll be damned."

They rode through the balance of the day. When dusk fell, they dismounted in order to see the tracks better, and having rested back at the willow-creek, as had their horses, they kept on walking, leading the animals.

Coolness arrived sometime after dark; the moon was slightly fuller, making it easier to see the tracks, although from the saddle this would not have been possible except in very soft places.

It was a long hike, something neither man was accustomed to, and again, Slade considered protesting, but one glance at the saloon-man's profile told him a protest would be useless. In any case, they were heading in the direction the blacksmith would have taken if he'd left his companion, and as long as they were doing that, Slade kept his protests to himself, except that now it was not the manhunt that bothered him, it was lack of sleep and food.

If he could have seen himself in a mirror his demoralization would have deepened. They hadn't shaved or adequately washed, their clothing was soiled and rumpled, their cheeks were sunken, and their eyes were red.

A stranger encountering them would probably have suspected they were fugitives not manhunters, but they did not see a soul until the following morning, about an hour after sunrise when they came around the flank of a hill and saw a shack with a small makeshift barn in the middle of nowhere.

There was a boxed-in dug well with the telltale beam above the hole and an old pulley on a rope leading to a bucket.

They surprised a thin, worn-looking woman with straggling graying hair as she came from the barn with a basket of eggs on one arm.

They were sitting their horses, still and silent. She stopped, and one hand flew to her mouth to stifle the scream as she faced them.

Slade spoke. He told her who they were and what they were doing — tracking a killer

243

— and that they would be glad to pay for some food, water, and a bait of hay for their animals.

She relaxed very gradually, glancing once toward the house. They dismounted and stood waiting. She finally told them there was timothy hay in the barn for their animals, and they could clean up and drink at the well while she was making a meal. She walked stiffly by.

They cared for the horses. Rourke took a bucket of water to the barn and sluiced off the back of his horse, and the blacksmith followed suit.

They cleaned up as best they could, drank deeply, and went to the house. When they knocked, the woman stepped aside. Behind her, a sweaty, haggard man sat on the side of a rumpled bed, holding a double-barreled scattergun. His unshaven face was sunken, his eyes were bright, and his hair was awry. He had been roused from the bed when the woman returned from the barn.

He was obviously ill, but there was nothing wrong with his voice. "Lay them guns on the table, gents. Do it real slow."

When Jim and Slade had obeyed, the man eased both dogs down on the shotgun and let it sag. The woman turned as the man began coughing. "That's my husband. He's

244

been poorly since last spring, but he seems to be gettin' better. Set, gents. I'll have breakfast ready real quick." She had fired up an old cast iron cookstove, and within minutes the inside of the one-room shack was like an oven. It was much hotter inside than it would be outside after the sun climbed.

The man had evidently exhausted his strength by sitting up and holding the shotgun; without another glance or word he sank back on the bed and closed his eyes.

Downing and Rourke noticed his shallow breathing. They had seen "lungers" before; this man was dying sure as hell, the galloping consumption killed them as surely as though they had been shot. It just took a lot longer.

By the time the woman placed food before them, both Slade and Jim were sweating. So was the woman. She was easier around them, finally, and apologized for the shack being so hot. Her husband got chilled very easily. They drank rank coffee and ate fried meat, which neither of them could identify, but the woman was clearly one of those natural cooks who could make fried rat taste good. No one could make the same claim for her coffee. It was black as midnight and strong enough to float horseshoes.

They asked about the shod-horse tracks passing down the north side of the little makeshift barn. She was surprised; she had seen no tracks.

They asked no additional questions. For one thing they were not only roasting, they were uncomfortable eating with that dying man and his labored breathing only about fifteen feet away.

They emptied their pockets on the table. The woman looked startled by the amount of money. As they were retrieving their weapons she said, "That's too much. I can't accept that. All I done was rassle together some —"

Rourke said, "Lady, it was worth every bit of that just to smell food again. Thank you an' good-bye."

Down at the barn an old swaybacked milk cow gazed stolidly at them. Neither Downing nor Rourke were stockmen, but they did not have to be to understand the reason for those deeply sunken places above the cow's eyes, the swayed back, the big paunch with ribs showing above it. The old girl was very elderly; if she gave much milk it was probably no more than the squatters got from day to day with none left over to make butter or cheese.

For once Slade was pleased to be a-horseback again. A mile farther along under the climbing sun he made an observation. "Why in the lord's name do people do that? Come

246

way out here and homestead. All you got to do is look around; the grass don't get tall, creeks for waterin' vegetable patches is far off, the wind must blow through here like hell . . . Why?"

Rourke, feeling as benign as he could under the circumstances, riding through the early day with those tracks clear as glass, mumbled something about hope springing eternal in the human heart, or something like that, and although the blacksmith still talked, Rourke tuned him out completely.

After a while Slade gazed at his companion. What in the world could drive a man like this manhunt was driving his old friend? He'd known James Rourke a long time; they had gone fishing in the mountains together, they had sat till midnight at poker sessions, they had held more leisurely discussions about everything from politics to religion than he could recall; in the end he decided, at least in this case incorrectly, that folks only thought they knew other folks, and lapsed in a silence that lingered until past midday when once again they halted at a creek to tank up and rest for a few minutes.

The ranch horses were holding up well, but there had never been much comparison between working stock horses and livery barn animals.

The horses they had acquired from that big cowman back yonder were muscled up, tough as boiled owls, and accustomed to instant obedience. They were a pleasure to ride if that had been all their present riders had to dwell upon, which it wasn't.

By midafternoon the men drooped, but the stock horses neither dragged in back nor acted as though what was being required of them was any different from what they had learned to live with since they had left the hackamore and acquired the bit.

Rourke knelt at their last halt in tree-shade to crumble dirt where the shod-horse imprints showed plainly. The soil was only slightly caked from heat, beneath the top layer the earth was faintly moist from dew. He arose to make this observation to the blacksmith, who had been watching glumly.

"He's not too far ahead, Slade. I guess he stopped for a while last night."

Instead of nodding about this, Downing said, "Where did you learn that business about the ground around a hoofprint?"

Rourke was swinging back across leather when he replied. "I never learned it, but after examinin' those tracks for as long as we been at it, it seemed pretty clear that with hot sun on the ground, anywhere there was a

248

deep impression, if the ground was still soft beneath . . ."

They continued until dusk. Rourke would have pushed on until dark, but his companion balked. They went to a shaded barranca, rode down into it, and no sooner had the blacksmith cared for his animal than he sank down in a rocky place with this eyes closed almost before his body turned loose.

Rourke prowled in search of water and found none. He was beyond the confines of where he had ever been before; saloonmen were town inhabitants. He had done some riding over the countryside but not in a westerly direction.

He walked back, listened to Slade's stentorian breathing, prowled over the tracks that had turned out and around the canyon, and followed them a short distance on foot before turning back.

The elusive man they were hunting was now heading directly toward Calabasas, even though that didn't make a lick of sense.

Rourke sat down in the grass and again was unaware of anything until a pack rat half as large as a cat flicked him in the face with its tail as it scampered across his chest.

He sat up. The rat, startled by movement, fled faster than it seemed its short legs could carry it. Rourke gazed at Slade. He looked

like hell; a rough guess was that big, mus-
cled-up Slade Downing had shrunk about ten
pounds since they had struck out. Rourke
felt sorry for the blacksmith. Maybe someday
he would explain why he was so driven to
catch the man on the big bay horse. Then
again, maybe he never would. If he explained
everything, Slade would do exactly what any
other normal human being would do, he
would start avoiding Rourke, watching him
from the corner of his eyes, and privately
pity him for functioning one brick shy of a
load.

When he awakened the blacksmith, Downing sat up slowly, rubbed his eyes, said his
tongue was as thick as a double saddle blanket, and looked around at Rourke. "Why is
this crazy son of a bitch goin' back toward
town?"

Instead of answering immediately Rourke
went after his horse. As they were rigging
out again he said, "I got no idea, but I'll
tell you for a fact, I'm glad he is, because
my butt's so sore I'll be settin' on pillows
for a week after we get back. How about
you?"

Downing did not answer. He climbed across
the leather, gave his friend a resigned look,
and followed in Rourke's wake exactly as he
had been doing for more weary hours than

he wanted to recall.

Halcón *had* stopped. They came upon his meager camp near one of those meandering creeks. They swung off to silently stand gazing at the ground where flattened grass showed where a large horse had rolled and where the horse had grazed on the moist green grass. Slade sighed. "Don't that man ever sleep?"

Rourke too saw no sign of a body having pressed down the grass. All he said was, "Well, at least his horse needs rest and feed sometime. I was beginning to think the horse, like the man . . ."

Downing did not wait for a conclusion to Jim's sentence. "By my guess we're about maybe twenty miles from town. Jim, when we get back, before I take a bath, shave, or even sleep, I'm goin' to want a gallon of beer an' a full peppermint stick."

Rourke smiled. "On the house. Let's go. I'd like to reach town by sunup tomorrow."

As they rode away from their prey's meager camp, Rourke puzzled about why the killer was returning to the place where he had definitely killed at least one man, and maybe even another two.

It did not really begin to worry him until sundown, when Slade wanted to stop. He figured that with about five to eight miles still to go, they could reach town in the morning, before the heat arrived.

Rourke waited until they found water and trees, then off saddled, washed the horse's back, hobbled the critter, upended his saddle in grass, and sat staring in the direction of Calabasas.

Up until now he had been obsessed with the chase, but unless Halcón rode around and past Calabasas, the town was most likely his destination, and *that* worried the saloonman.

The business of a killer was to kill, bushwhack, stand up and face down, whatever was required, but kill. If Halcón stopped in Calabasas . . . Not only *if* he stopped there, but *why,* when he knew he was being chased and had to know for a damned fact the community by now had an identification of the back shooter who had killed Marshal Butts, would he run the risk of being recognized?

The answer came logically and very unpleasantly: because he was not through killing; there was someone else in Calabasas he meant to murder.

Slade was snoring like an asthmatic bull. Rourke looked around at the blacksmith lying on rocks, sound asleep.

He might as well rest, too; as Slade had observed, they could reach town by midmorning. As he searched for a place free of stones to settle down, he had an odd sensation of reluctance about getting back.

Dog-tired men do not analyze, even if they ordinarily do, and the whisker-stubbled, worn-out men resting amid rocks were neither analytical by nature — nor inclined to heed premonitions.

19

Tired Men

When they had Calabasas in sight Rourke was struck by a thought. There was no question that Halcón, leaving a trail to be followed and having covered the same ground his pursuers had covered with abundant points of observation along the way, had watched the blacksmith and the saloonman. Why hadn't he bushwhacked them? He was certainly capable of bushwhacking — the hangrope ruse had worked perfectly as had the map that led Henry Drake to his death.

As they slouched along, sunken-eyed, mostly silent, not yet demoralized but certainly worn out, Rourke watched rooftops. Hell, if Halcón had meant to bushwhack them he could have done it a dozen places on the backtrail; he certainly would not attempt it in town.

But Jim Rourke was beginning to think of this entire affair in a different way — which he could never have explained to Slade, nor to anyone else for that matter. He was beginning to think in terms that throughout history had been called myths. For example that big thoroughbred-looking horse with the iron shoes: Slade had said iron horseshoes had stopped being used with the advent of the steam engine. Who would still be around to make shoes like that or fit them to a particular horse?

He asked Slade if he had fitted a pair of iron shoes and got a look that would have withered flowers if there had been any around. "I told you; I was a button when them things was almost completely gone from use."

"You're a smith, Slade. If someone come along to have iron shoes put on his horse, could you do it?"

"You mean could I make iron shoes? No — neither could any other blacksmith nowadays. They was forged, Jim, like iron parts for wagons and other things is forged . . . forged shoes can't be fitted to just any horse, you understand?"

"No."

"Well . . . what the hell are we talkin' about such a silly subject for? Iron shoes required the exact measurement of each hoof, you see? They had to be made for just one individual horse because if they had to be shaped at an anvil like we do now to get the best fit, it couldn't be done. You can heat cast iron until the cows come home an' it'll get cherry-red, but the minute you warp it over an anvil, it breaks. Cast iron is brittle, understand now?"

Rourke forced a smile, trying to soften the obvious irritation of his companion. He faced forward again and rode half the distance toward town in silence. Slade finally said, "If he stops in town he's crazy. Enough folks know about him by now from the store clerk. Someone will cut him down on sight."

Jim nodded. "An' suppose he rides out an' around town an' keeps going?"

Downing pressed both hands on the saddle horn and looked bleakly at his friend. "Then you follow him alone, partner."

Rourke was studying buildings up ahead with an expression of almost brooding discomfort. "He knew we was behind him."

Downing's reply was blunt. "Sure he did. What the hell — he had to. We followed his tracks across a lot of open country, out in plain sight."

"Then why didn't he try to ambush us?"

Downing was scratching inside his shirt and continued a while before answering. "Your guess is as good as mine."

"He's a killer, Slade."

"I know that."

"Then tell me why he led us all over hell, then came back to town, knowin' we was behind him and would also get to town — and tell folks what we knew?"

Slade stopped scratching and wrinkled his nose. They were still a fair distance from the outskirts, but aromas carried even farther on cool summertime mornings, and there was definitely a scent of cooking breakfast meat and coffee in the air.

"Why, Slade?"

"Why, what?"

"Why did he let us shag him back to town without doin' what he seems to do best — bushwhack us?"

"Jim — how the hell would I know? Right now I itch all over, my belly's so shrunk it's hooked over a bone in my spine, I'm thirsty, tired as hell, and as far as I'm concerned, this crazy man can stop in town or keep on ridin' easterly until he's invisible."

One possibility hit Jim Rourke like a rock. He slouched along, pondering it. It was not a very complicated notion; in fact he probably should have wondered about it before.

If that ratty old harness maker really had seen someone skulking out back of his shop across from the saloon, and if that skulker had been spying on the saloon through the roadway window, he would have seen Rourke sitting at that table reading the newspaper, his back to the window to get light to see by. Rourke had done that several times. The one time *someone else* had done it, a bushwhacker from behind the harness works had shot him.

Rourke came slowly out of his weariness. *He was the one who was supposed to have been killed!*

He made an exclamation that brought Downing's head around. "Son of a bitch!"

They were too near the west side of town with its tantalizing scents for the blacksmith to be interested in his companion's abrupt exclamation. In fact, about ten yards before they reached the west-side alley Downing was already beginning to rein toward the lower end of town where he could leave the horse at Jobey's barn, after which all he had to do was head for his bed. Food could come later, as could that promised load of beer at the saloon.

Rourke watched his friend angle away toward the livery barn without a word passing between them. He understood; he even sympathized. For himself, he did not take the borrowed horse to Jobey's barn because, for one reason, he knew Alex would be down there with a whole herd of questions. Slade could take care of that; knowing Slade as well as he did he knew what Slade's reaction would be when the questions started — a mean look, no words as the blacksmith headed home.

He took the horse over to the corralyard, where the young Mexican met him with an expression of surprise, but he said nothing as Rourke handed him the reins, asked him to see that the animal was cared for. He entered the saloon from out back, tossed his hat away, drank deeply of water in a ladle-bucket, blew out a shaky long breath, and went to sit on a bench behind his darkened bar.

Later he ate from the supply of free lunch kept beneath the bar for the evening trade, drank more water, went into his storeroom, made a pallet of old canvas, and stretched out with his eyes closed. But sleep would not come immediately.

Those iron horseshoe tracks had led straight into town. Halcón had indeed returned to Calabasas. He had not ridden around the town to continue riding. He had entered town by the same west-side alley Rourke and Downing had entered.

Sleep came before Rourke had finished his ponderings.

It was as dark as the inside of a well when he awakened, and the town was quiet — for a change not even a single dog was barking. Rourke went after more water, lighted a lamp, shaved with an old razor, removed his upper clothing, and returned to the canvas pallet, where he went back to sleep.

The next time he awakened, the town was noisily alive with both foot and horse traffic. He lay back until someone loudly rattled the roadway door. He arose, aware of aches in places he did not even know he had places.

He didn't open the saloon. Taking along some spare clothing, he went up the alley to the tonsorial parlor, startled the hell out of the barber, who had been dozing in his chair while awaiting customers, and paid two bits for a bar of brown soap, an old towel, and the key to the bathhouse out back.

He sat in warm water, still with no regard for time, until someone banged on the door and growled about anyone taking so long to get clean.

He toweled off, dressed, and opened the door. Alex Jobey was standing there, scowling. His scowl faded, replaced by an expression of total astonishment. Rourke nodded and brushed past on his way to return the towel and soap. The moment Rourke appeared, the barber said, "There's talk all over town that you'd been killed. Alex Jobey told me just a few minutes ago Slade Downing

260

came back lookin' like the wrath of gawd — alone, Alex said, so folks figured you'd been killed."

Rourke looked steadily at the barber. "Now you know different," he said, and walked out into bright sunlight. He unlocked the saloon from out front and went inside to where the roadway window with the small hole in it brightened the room.

He had scarcely got behind the bar before customers arrived. They didn't bother to call for drinks, just interrupted each other with questions. Rourke answered them all the same way. No, they hadn't caught the man who had killed Marshal Butts, but they had ridden themselves down to a nubbin in the effort. And no, they had never caught sight of him.

Walt Bellamy, dusty from a recent run, asked which way the murderer had gone. Jim said, "West, an' he had one hell of a horse under him."

Walt was satisfied. "West. Well, there's nothin' but cow outfits out there, which he can avoid real easy, so I guess we'll never see him again."

Rourke's reticence went unnoticed until late afternoon when Jem Dugan and John Bacon, the town carpenter, met down in front of the smithy, which was still locked tight, and reached a conclusion. Jem said, "Rourke's holdin' somethin' back."

Bacon eyed the flighty older man. "How d'you know that? You'n Rourke haven't spoken since Doc Williams got shot."

"Well — I know it because I've heard some of the fellers who been at the saloon said he don't talk much."

The carpenter looked down his nose at the wiry, shorter man. "Jem, if you just got back from two days an' better sittin' on a damned horse I got an idea you'd be tired clean through, too. Men don't talk much when they been drug out for a couple of days . . . Well, maybe except you, an' I suspect your tongue is hinged in the middle and wags at both ends."

The insulted harness maker stamped all the way across the road before turning in the direction of his shop.

But he had been right, rumor or not; Jim Rourke had not been the same since returning to town as he had been before riding out.

Pete Bradley, the hard-of-hearing pool-hall proprietor, arrived as the late-day saloon trade was dwindling. Rourke had nothing particular against Bradley, except that when he was at the bar he talked too loud and was invariably answered the same way.

Pete wanted to know if Slade Downing was all right, because his smithy was still locked and a freighter who had hauled hides up to the tanyard wanted to get some mules reshod.

"Go rattle the door to his shack out back. He might still be asleep," Rourke advised loudly.

Bradley frowned. "I already done that. No one come to the door."

Rourke swabbed his bartop as he said what he did not believe. "Then maybe he's not around. Maybe he's gone somewhere."

Bradley looked annoyed. "An' who in the hell," he shouted, "is goin' to do blacksmithing? His place's been locked up for over three days."

Rourke asked if he would like a beer. Bradley shook his head and stamped out of the saloon.

Rourke drew off a beer for himself. He would have bet new money Slade was either still sleeping, or was maybe eating, in either case, knowing Slade Downing as he did, Rourke was satisfied that if he had been inside, he was not yet ready to meet folks, something Rourke could understand.

The store clerk came in, acting as diffident as always. He smiled and asked for beer, which Rourke drew off and set in front of him. Amos had a question, but it was not at all what Rourke expected. He leaned on the bar, drank half his beer, and said quietly,

"I been runnin' the store like always, Mister Rourke, an' I got somethin' I'd like to ask you.

"I been putting the money in the office safe like Mister Drake did, an' now it's got to be quite a bit of cash. . . . Did Mister Drake have kin? I can't just keep runnin' the store, it don't belong to me. If he had kin they should be notified he's dead. Did you ever hear him say — ?"

"Never," Rourke replied, anticipating the rest of the question. "I never heard him mention any relatives. Maybe someone else around town who was closer to him than I was might know."

The clerk finished his beer and pushed the glass away. "I've asked. They all say about the same as you said."

"Go through the papers in his office, Amos."

"I did that. There's bills of lading and whatnot goin' back to when he first run the business, but nothin' personal."

"Try his house. If he had personal papers they'd most likely be there."

The clerk showed immediately he had not liked that suggestion. "I can't do that. It'd be like burglarizin' the place."

Rourke wanted to sigh; instead he gave his opinion of the clerk's reluctance. "Amos, you

264

worked for Henry for a long time. You knew him better'n anyone else. If you don't find out whether he had kin or not, take my word for it no one else is going to. No one else really liked Henry that much."

The timid man nodded agreement. He had not liked Mister Drake very much either, but he had worked for him, had taken his money, and therefore felt uneasy about prying where he knew Mister Drake would never have tolerated prying. He paid for his beer and left the saloon, no less troubled than when he had entered it.

Someone was banging on the alley door. Rourke went back and opened it. Slade slid past without a word. Someone out front was rapping the bar with an empty glass. Rourke pointed toward the door to his storeroom, said he would return as quickly as he could, and hastened forward to care for his noisy customer.

Because it was close to supper time he was unable to return to the storeroom for more than an hour, was not in fact sure Slade would still be there.

There was still one man at the bar, Enos Jordan, Alex Jobey's rather dim but good-natured hostler. Enos never, or at least very rarely, had enough money for more than one drink. Otherwise, even the old men who ordinarily whiled away hot afternoons playing matchstick poker over beyond the woodstove at a big round table had departed not long before.

Rourke risked losing a few customers; his regulars would not return until after supper when dusk would be deepening into night.

He went back to the storeroom. The reason Slade had not departed full of impatience was because he was stretched full length on the canvas pallet, sound asleep.

Rourke gazed at the blacksmith, who had shaved but was still attired in the same filthy clothing he had returned to town in. Rourke went back out front. Even the hostler was gone. He got a bottle and a glass and returned to the storeroom.

Slade awakened like a bear with a sore behind. He glared, growled, eventually realized where he was and who had interrupted his sleep, sat up, and rubbed his eyes as he said, "Every gawddamned horse that was ever borned wore out his shoes while I was gone. I got blessed out by half the town for not bein' handy to shoe someone's animal."

Rourke offered the glass and bottle. Slade ignored the glass, swallowed twice, and held the bottle away as he snorted like a bay steer and shook all over. Rourke took back the bottle as the blacksmith fixed him with an indignant stare. "If I ever go manhuntin' with you again, I hope the lord strikes me dead!"

Rourke nodded. "Me too."

Slade overlooked that remark "Do you know where them iron tracks went?"

"Back into town from the same side we come back."

"Well, are you goin' to just set there? That son of a bitch is back among us. We got to organize a search. We got to find him an' hang him so high the birds'll nest in his hair."

Rourke considered the bottle he was holding. "That might not be real smart, Slade. He's a real good bushwhacker."

"He's not good enough to bushwhack the whole town!"

Rourke raised his eyes to the other man's face. "I wouldn't bet money on that, partner."

20

A Near Thing

Father Cordero de la Cruz was sitting out back in near darkness with a glass of red wine, when he heard boot steps approaching.

The approaching shadow greeted him in Spanish. "Good day, Father."

The priest offered no correction — it was nighttime, not daytime. He patted the seat of a very old bench. *"Sentar, compañero."* The priest arose to get another mug of wine. When he returned, Rourke had placed his hat beside him on the bench and had shoved his legs out. He was peering out where there had been a mound and a hole and where now there was neither. He did not mention the filled-in grave, saying instead, "Well, you know he shot the town marshal."

"Yes . . . Do you know what I thought about that, friend? I thought he had little reason to kill that one."

Rourke sipped wine. "Father, he's after me

as sure as we're sitting here."

"Why you?"

"Who knows?" Rourke replied, then launched into an explanation. When he had finished, the priest said nothing for a long time. Of course the saloonman could be right — but why? Well, right or wrong . . . The priest lay a hand on Rourke's arm. "He is here again."

"Yes. We followed him. He rode west for many miles, turned half around for a while, then faced east and rode all the way back to town."

The priest sighed. "His work is not done then."

"His name is Halcón."

The priest shrugged without comment. His name could be anything he chose to make it. He had used more names over periods of time than anyone really knew about.

"I need advice, Father. But first, tell me — just how does he do all these things that a man would do?"

"When he takes a form, as the old man they called The Toothless One did, he sacrifices some of the things — Let me say it another way. As a man, he cannot go beyond the powers of men. He becomes one of us. You understand?"

Rourke did not reply. He sat awhile in thought, then when he spoke again, his voice sounded less troubled and tired.

"Maybe, maybe not. The town blacksmith an' I rode ourselves hard an' we still had to rest an' drink water an' eat."

"Well, but companion, these things he has never done, has never needed to do. You see?"

"No, I don't see, but I know what we saw, so I'll not mention that. It answers a question to which I already have the answer, Father . . . Little by little I'm making sense from all this."

"Good. Very good, friend," the priest said. "However, these are things to be discussed later, no? If you believe he is going to kill you, let me tell you, companion, he never sleeps, he never eats, he has waited lifetimes. Even longer."

Rourke looked at the smaller, dark man. "I am a dead man, Father?"

The priest's discomfort was obvious even in darkness.

The Spanish language avoids bluntness. From this comes an inhibition about blunt statements. Father Cordero de la Cruz was also a holy man, so he had two, rather than one, inhibitions. He was orthodox; orthodoxy taught that life was precious, one

270

might even say sacred.

"Padre . . . ?"

"Friend, I can tell you he does not always succeed. I told you, when he arrives appearing as human as everyone else, he must rely on slyness — centuries of experience in how to accomplish his end, *as a person.* He has not always succeeded."

Rourke squinted in the direction of the old graveyard. "But he *does* succeed."

The priest fell silent again for several moments. He finished his red wine and put the glass aside. "What I can tell you is that since we know who he is, you have some advantage, but remember, he has been doing this for so long. Well, men *have* outsmarted him because when he appears as one of us he has to function as we function. Those are his restraints."

Rourke sighed aloud. "The chance of a snowball in hell, Father?"

Father Cordero de la Cruz shifted on the bench before speaking again. When he spoke, he did not answer the question. He instead said, "This I know from my schooling. When men hunt him, he can detect their approach. The times I have read that he failed was when men waited for him to come to them. *He* can detect *you,* but *you* cannot detect *him.* Companion, if he is indeed coming to kill you, he has many ways of using your inability to guard against his arrival."

"Big odds, Father. Do you know what he can and cannot do?"

"Yes. One thing. If you move into the church he cannot kill you without entering inside to do it, which he has never done . . . and for a very good reason. Holy places are sanctified ground."

"How long would I stay in the mission?"

"That, companion, I cannot say. Remember what I told you — he can wait a lifetime. He can wait several lifetimes."

Rourke frowned slightly. "Many thanks for your offer, if that is what it was, but for a certainty I cannot sit in there for a lifetime, can I?"

"It has been done, companion."

"In New Mexico, Father?"

"I cannot say about New Mexico, but elsewhere. There are stories from times past —"

"Pardon me, Father, we are sitting here talking about one chance in what — five hundred? Maybe one thousand?"

The little priest mopped sweat off his forehead, and it was not a warm night under the old overhang. A faint breeze was blowing the full length of it from north to south.

"Who can say, friend? Maybe that many chances, maybe many less." The priest arose.

"One thing — If you have reason to believe he is getting close, you must come swiftly to the mission."

Rourke arose, dumped his hat on, and gazed at the shorter man. "I appreciate what you are saying, friend, but how many times could I reach here before he killed me? And while I am full of gratitude for your offer, Father, I have never been a good runner."

The priest said, "I have already said at the altar I think he is here. Now I will say I *know* he is here. I go now to ask for an interdiction. Good night, my friend, and God be with you."

On the way back to Gringo-town it did not occur to Jim Rourke he could be getting lined up through someone's sights, but he arrived at the saloon and got inside without incident.

He doused the lights, barred the door from the inside, groped his way through darkness to find a bottle and glass behind the bar, and sat on a stool, drinking slowly and from time to time wagging his head.

Of all the unbelievable, downright impossible things to happen to a man who ran a saloon in a cowtown in a place called New Mexico, which wasn't even defined on many maps, this had to be the most baffling.

Why hadn't the killer shot him while

Rourke and Slade Downing were shagging him? Not because he did not know he was being shagged, and probably not because he had not recognized Rourke as one of his pursuers. Then why?

Jim downed a jolt and breathed heavily for a moment. The little priest, whose name meant Lamb of the Cross, had clearly wanted to be hopeful and just as clearly was not very hopeful at all.

One chance, Rourke thought, and felt the whiskey because he had not eaten lately. He felt less elated from the liquor than tired, so he did as he had done before: went to the storeroom and slept on the layers of old canvas.

Morning arrived with an abrupt blaze of brilliance that brightened the inside of the saloon as far as the backbar even though Rourke's saloon faced west.

Rourke cleaned up, left the roadway door locked, and went down to the cafe by the back alley. The hour was late for early diners, but there were still a few dawdlers loafing away the digestive process with coffee and conversation.

Rourke was greeted with solemn nods, a few smiles, and several looks of bafflement. It had become local knowledge that both the saloonman and the blacksmith had returned to Calabasas very different from the two men who had ridden out, but Rourke particularly. He seemed to be preoccupied even while tending his bar; he was genial, still joked with customers, but his smile lacked warmth, seemed almost mechanical.

He *was* different, men said, and inevitably speculated until some very bizarre rumors blossomed into full-blown gossip.

Several days passed, the heat increased and became once more the prime topic around town, and the story of the tan-hided stranger who had killed Marshal Butts was well on the way to oblivion when an unfortunate event occurred.

A dusky-skinned 'breed of some kind, part Indian or part Mex, drove a freight wagon to the northern edge of town up near the tanyard and set up camp where other freighters had camped for years.

He went down to the mercantile for tobacco, baking soda, a small sack of flour, and a box of six-gun ammunition.

It was the box of bullets that bothered Amos Lawton more than the man's looks, which as he remembered them fitted the opinion of how the murderer had looked.

He tended the store until evening. After locking up he went first to the cafe, where during the course of some general conversation he mentioned the freighter and his suspicion. After that he drifted up to the saloon. Here, his story, spoken quietly, turned the otherwise somewhat noisy room deeply silent. Rourke leaned on the bar as he said, "A freighter . . . with a wagon and teams an' a load?"

Amos nodded.

Rourke continued to gaze at the clerk until a gruff-voiced townsman farther up the bar made a growly suggestion.

"Well now, that don't jibe, does it? That coppery feller was a-horseback."

"Maybe," squeaked another customer at the bar in an almost girlish voice. "Maybe he stole the outfit somewhere. Maybe he's real *coyote* and —"

Rourke interrupted the man with the girlish voice. "For a fact he's always been a-horseback before. Why should he change to a wagon? Someone ought to go talk to him. Most likely he's what he claims to be, a freighter."

Walt Bellamy volunteered. "I know most of them freighters. I'll talk to him."

Squeaky-voice said, "Take a hangrope along, Walt, just in case."

No one laughed.

After the whip departed, Pete Bradley, who had followed the discussion with a hand behind one ear, put aside a half-empty beer glass and turned away from the bar. "I'll go with him. Just in case," he announced loudly. This time someone did laugh. It was a stocky rangeman who wore his spurs down a notch so that when he walked they sounded musical — to him anyway.

Before the cowboy got clear of the bar, or Pete Bradley reached the spindle doors, Rourke said, "Not you, Pete." He had to repeat it louder. *"Not you, Pete!"*

Bradley and the cowboy turned. The pool-hall proprietor looked quizzical, but the rangeman's face was smoothly expressionless. He seemed to think the shout had been directed at him. He gazed without blinking at the man behind the bar until the town carpenter spoke directly to him.

"It's a personal matter, son. Mister Rourke is right. It wouldn't be a good idea for a deaf man and a young buck wearing a gun to go talk to that feller."

Bradley returned to the bar. He had not made out the carpenter's words, but he had heard Rourke perfectly.

The cowboy, with every eye on him, gave it up and also returned to the bar.

Nothing was resolved. Later, when Rourke looked for the store clerk, he was not in the saloon. When the last of his customers had departed, Rourke had one on the house.

Naw, that wouldn't be *him*. For a fact the entire Southwest was inhabited by 'breeds of every shade and mixture. Miscegenation, known by Rourke and everyone he knew by a different name, had been going on for more than a hundred years.

But the idea was firmly in the back of Rourke's mind. As he was cleaning up after locking the roadway door he recalled some of the priest's words. Father Cordero de la Cruz had said emphatically that when *he* appeared as a man, for as long as he was in that guise he was bound to function as a man.

Well, Halcón was a man all right, and he was known as a horseman. There was a bare chance the freighter was Halcón, but Rourke did not believe he was.

He decided to investigate for himself. His concern made one thing abundantly clear. The townsmen of Calabasas wanted a killer; wanted someone's blood.

By the time Rourke reached the wagon camp north of town, there were at least ten torches. He saw the townsmen long before he saw the terrified 'breed with his back to the fore-wheel of an old freight wagon.

The young man was not only terrified, he had clearly been surprised when the lynch mob reached him. Halcón would not have

278

been caught by surprise.

Rourke came up from the rear. He knew every man there. Jem Dugan was almost dancing with anticipation as he yelled for men to hoist the wagon tongue, which was how hangings were accomplished in a more-or-less treeless country.

Rourke's anger rose as he punched his way to the front of the crowd, where the harness maker was jabbing at the terrified freighter. The 'breed looked to be no more than perhaps twenty-five.

Rourke grabbed Dugan by the shoulder, spun him around, and knocked him flat. All movement stopped. The silence was adequate for the sound of hissing greasewood torches to be heard.

Rourke stood wide-legged. "You damned idiots! This is not the gunman! I know him by sight. He looks older an' he's darker."

The armed crowd stared. Someone helped the harness maker to his feet, but he had to be supported or he would have fallen. Rourke turned toward the sweating freighter and asked him in Spanish what his name was.

The younger man shook his head. "I don't know no Mex."

Rourke switched to English. "What's your name?"

"Alfred Solus. I been freightin' for two years. I never hauled freight down here before."

"Do you know what the Spanish word *halcón* means?"

"Mister, I'm half Portygee. I don't talk nothin' but English an' a little Portygee. I got no idea what that word means."

Rourke turned. Already several of the lynch mob had departed. He shook his head at the others. "Do you gents agree we need a lawman?"

Every head nodded.

Rourke nodded too as he said, "If for no better reason than to keep you damned fools from murdering someone you never saw before an' know nothin' about. Go on home. Tomorrow, drinks on the house. An' take that old scarecrow with you."

One of the men supporting Jem Dugan said, "I think you busted his jaw."

Rourke glared. "Good. Then the mouthy old rattle-brained son of a bitch won't be able to talk for a while."

As the last few townsmen started back the way they had come, torches smoking, Rourke faced the young 'breed, who gave him no chance to speak first.

"Mister, thank god you come . . . I'll never haul another thing to this town. Not even water if folks is dyin' of thirst!"

Rourke smiled and said nothing. There really wasn't much to be said anyway. He slapped the younger man on the shoulder and trudged back into town.

21

A Solitary Night Rider

For the second time since spring, Rourke's trade was off by at least half. Also for the second time, his customers returned gradually, sheepishly. Rourke greeted them as though there had not been a near-lynching, an attitude that was met with relief. The subject was never again mentioned in the saloon. Throughout town, of course, there was talk, but not much; none of the almost lynchers were willing to make statements that made them look bad.

The hardest pill to swallow was for the harness maker to explain the lump on the side of his jaw. Because he now thoroughly disliked Jim Rourke, where before he had only resented him, he got red in the face as he told a lie about bumping into something in the dark. Of course, in time the truth became known, but most folks were content to let a sleeping dog lie.

Three days after the young freighter harnessed up, delivered his freight in record time, and drove away without even looking back, Walt Bellamy came in off a southbound run from Evansville, thirty miles north, dry as dust. He drank water at the corralyard, then made a beeline for Rourke's place to take up the slack in his thirst with something that had more muscle.

It had been hot lately, increasingly so over the past few days. Folks kept watching for the thunderheads that usually came in behind scorching heat, but this time there were no clouds, just heat so bad folks could have used rocks to cook on.

Walt groaned about the heat, not necessarily for himself — he had lived with heat all his life — but for the horses that had to sweat bucketsful to keep the stages more or less on schedule.

There was one consolation: in summertime stagecoaches were used, much lighter vehicles than the big, heavy, winter mud wagons with tires four inches wide.

Rourke shrugged about that. "The horses don't sweat as much in winter, Walt."

Bellamy downed his beer, chewed his peppermint, and nodded for a refill. He was, in spite of tanking up on water at the yard, just beginning to sweat hard, which required more beer.

As Jim returned with the thick, large glass, Walt beat off dust, ran a scarred hand through his scanty hair, and said he had heard of the lynching attempt. He hoisted the glass in a small salute, half drained it, and wiped his mouth on a dirty sleeve before speaking again. "You done a good turn, Jim."

"Jem Dugan don't think so."

"Jem Dugan never had a thought of any kind. By the way, you know where them old In'ian ruins is, out quite a ways from town an' maybe west of the stage road, five, maybe six miles?"

Rourke nodded. Once, years back, he had ridden out there, found nothing to excite his interest, and returned to town. Some folks pawed the ground, dug into graves, got all excited about those things. Rourke had seen a dozen in his lifetime. They all looked the same, eroded down to globs of mud — forlorn, unpleasant places.

Bellamy mopped his face with a blue bandana. "Well, it was about even with them ruins but on the road when my only passenger, a drummer from Denver, had to take a piss, so I stopped. While he was behind the coach I got down to check the horses . . . There was some shod-horse tracks leadin' from the road west toward that old ruin."

Rourke nodded, knowing more was coming and waiting for it. Bellamy drained the thick glass and pushed it away as he resumed speaking. "Now I'm no blacksmith, but I've been around shod horses most of my life, an' when shoes get worn, they show it. These here tracks was so clear I could make out the worn-down nail heads."

Rourke nodded again. "New shoes, Walt."

"No, let me finish. They wasn't new shoes, partner. They was wore smooth."

Rourke's brow began to gather into a frown. "The nail heads was worn flat but the shoes wasn't?"

"Yep. All the way back to town I figured on that."

Rourke was looking straight at the whip. "How clear were those tracks?"

"I just told you, clear as any tracks I've ever seen. They wasn't new shoes and the imprint was slick from wear but not really worn down. More like iron than steel."

Rourke went to draw off two beers, one of which he set before the stager. They both half drained the glasses before Rourke asked another question. "How fresh would you say they were?"

Bellamy replied shortly. "Well, I can't say for a fact, except that if a man could make 'em out clear, they couldn't have been real old, could they?"

Rourke drank slowly. When his glass was empty he asked the whip how he got along with his new boss. Rourke could not have struck upon a better way to change the subject. Bellamy smiled broadly. "He's young, but he's decent to get along with. The last bossin' job he had was in Nebraska, where he said it rains often durin' summer. I think the heat bothers him, but hell, given enough time he'll make out. One hell of an improvement over — say, has anyone heard from Martin Bedford? You know, when he disappeared he was ridin' a company animal, an' since he never come back, that's horse stealing."

The conversation drifted among several topics before Walt departed. Rourke greeted his next customers in a preoccupied manner, which they probably thought was no different than it had been since he and Slade had returned from that wild goose chase. At least no one commented at first, but once when Rourke went to his storeroom for another bottle, a few words passed among his customers. Some simply rolled their eyes and shook their heads.

That night, with customers lined up like crows on a fence, Jim took Alex Jobey to one side and asked him if he had a horse who would come home if left by himself.

Alex had several. All but one were barn-sour; they would go maybe as far as the north end of town, then balk, and unless their rider was knowledgeable about barn-sour horses and whanged hell out of them, they would turn around, and no amount of seesawing on the bit would deter them. They would bring the rider — usually red-faced and cussing — back to the barn.

Rourke listened to all this, then asked about the one horse that wasn't barn-sour.

It was a mare. Alex said she was a real problem every twenty-eight days when she was horsing, but otherwise she was a nice riding animal. Alex said he would sell her for exactly what he had paid — fifteen dollars — just to have peace among the geldings. He also said he had been half-drunk when he'd bought her and that if he'd been sober the seller couldn't have given her to him. Alex was a horseman. Real horsemen had little use for mares.

Rourke treated the liveryman to a drink, got busy among his other customers; when he returned to the section of the bar where the liveryman had been, there were silver coins beside an empty glass.

An old cowman leaning near the empty

space watched Rourke scoop up the coins and said, "Y'know, I been thinkin' lately of sellin' out, movin' to some town, an' gettin' into the livery business. Alex always looks well fed." The cowman peered into his empty jolt glass and shoved it over for Rourke to refill it. "My wife don't think much of the idea. She says I don't have the right temperment for dealin' with the public."

Rourke smiled, nodded, and went to fill some other empty glasses. It was a long evening, and it was well along toward becoming a long night too. Usually only Saturday nights ran on into the wee hours.

Slade Downing came in, looking as though he had bathed recently and changed into spanking-clean clothing. When he settled into the space Alex Jobey had left, the old cowman wrinkled his nose, considered the blacksmith for a moment, then said, "Slade, you been out to the city, have you?"

Downing was puzzled. "No, not for three, four years. Why?"

"Well — now we been friends a long time — well, you smell like you been to one of them fancy houses in the city."

Downing was nonplussed, but only very briefly. "It's that danged barber. Some travelin' man sold him a crate of what he says is French toilet water. When he finishes

shavin' an' cuttin', he sprinkles some of that stuff on. Lilac rose, he calls it."

The cowman nodded. "Good thing you ain't married, Slade. If I come home smellin' like that, my wife'd brain me with an iron skillet."

Slade caught Rourke's gaze and nodded. When the bottle and glass arrived, Slade refilled the old rancher's glass first, then his own. The stockman muttered appreciation for the drink and headed for the door. He had a twelve mile ride ahead and if he reached home feeling as he did now, for a fact he'd face that iron fry-pan, so he let the horse poke along on a loose rein at a slow walk.

It wasn't much before the cowman reached home before Rourke bid the last customer good-night and barred the roadway door after him.

He'd been formulating a scheme since he'd listened to Walt Bellamy. He was normally not a man who went looking for trouble, and he was mindful of the priest's advice: let Halcón come to him; don't go to Halcón because in some way the priest hadn't explained, Halcón knew when an enemy was approaching.

That was all well and good, but this damned business could go on for weeks or maybe even months, with Halcón maneuvering into

a bushwhacking position. Rourke was not going to sit and wait, even though the priest had advised it and as far as Jim knew, Father Cordero de la Cruz was the only individual anywhere around who had any knowledge at all of what Halcón represented.

Jim shoved an old six-gun into his front waistband, took his Winchester, left the saloon by the back alley, went south in darkness until he was abreast of Alex's barn, then crossed over. He saw no one and assumed no one saw him. It was very late.

Alex was home in bed, the nightman said, and looked wonderingly at the saloonman loaded for bear. Jim asked about a mare Alex had told him wasn't barn-sour but knew her way home.

The nighthawk nodded. "Miss Muffet. It ain't her name. I don't know what her name is. That's what I call her."

"Bring her in and rig her out."

The nighthawk stared. "Now, Mister Rourke? You know about what time it is?"

Rourke leaned the carbine aside. "I know what time it is. Bring her in. I'll help with the saddling."

While the hostler went after the mare, Jim leaned in the front doorway looking up through town. For all he knew, this might be the last time he'd see Calabasas.

The town had been good to him; he liked it and most of the people in it. If he hadn't liked less the idea of getting shot in the back next week, next month, or a year from now, he would not be leaving it tonight.

The idea of waiting for an experienced bushwhacker to come to him hadn't set well with him, even when the priest suggested that he do it. Ed Ballinger and Henry Drake were fair examples of what happened when folks waited for Halcón to come to them, except that he doubted very much that either the marshal or the merchant had any idea they were being baited to their deaths. Rourke thought that, for a fact, he had to give the devil his due.

The nighthawk appeared. Without speaking, he and Rourke rigged out the animal, and because Rourke had no saddle boot for the Winchester, the nighthawk brought an old one from the harness room, buckled it into place, and stood back as Rourke upended his carbine for it to slide into the sheath.

Rourke said nothing to the nighthawk; he was only thinking ahead. The nighthawk watched Jim go north to the upper end of town on the roadway, and turned away only after Rourke was no longer in sight.

When he told Mister Jobey in the morning about the saloonman hiring a horse and riding out only two, three hours before sunrise, Mister Jobey was going to be interested.

It was a long ride on a beautiful night. Stars shone like diamonds flung randomly across the heavens by a giant hand.

The mare was short backed, close coupled, walked right along, and minded her own business. She was a sort of strawberry roan color. Clearly, she had been born with a nice disposition.

Rourke was a third of the way when an unpleasant thought struck him. Suppose Halcón couldn't be killed by bullets?

Jim had been taught as a small child that personified evil was indestructible regardless of what form or nature it appeared in.

He had not been inside a church further back than he could remember, nor was he convinced right now, on his way to kill a murderer, if there was any way to successfully do it, that what Sunday school teachers had taught him as a child had any relevance to what he was involved in now.

He clung to just one thing: Father Cordero de la Cruz had said the man he wanted to kill was subject to the same limitations and constraints other men were.

Rourke hoped very hard this was true, because although Halcón might in some way

292

have to behave as other men, would he have attributes other than being able to know when an enemy was coming to him? For example, would Halcón know a man he had tried to shoot in the back through a window was coming to look for him with guns? Would he laugh because he had faced guns before and was still around?

The priest had said Halcón would know an enemy was approaching. The closer he got to the area where he would leave the road to ride westward, the more he cleared all doubts and misgivings from his mind to concentrate on why he was out here in the night.

Back in town, the plan he was embarking on had seemed to have elements of success. Riding westerly now toward the confrontation he expected to occur, doubts about success increased. He was not going up against any run-of-the-mill gunman. He blocked out those thoughts, too.

He could not dwell on negatives; to stand any chance at all against Halcón he would need every bit of concentration he possessed. Maybe more, maybe one hell of a lot more.

If he never returned his disappearance would probably be classified right up there with the disappearance of Martin Bedford. People would know he had ridden out of town very late at night, armed for trouble. If, as he had planned, the "homing" roan mare returned without her rider, conjecture would just naturally flourish, but whether he was ever found or not, the specters of Anasazi Pueblo, if there were such things, would know his secret. He had told no one, neither Father Cordero de la Cruz nor the skeptical Slade Downing, the only two who might be concerned.

The priest would have an inkling if Rourke's riderless horse returned, but since he was inhibited about Gringo-town, and was by nature a reticent individual, the riddle of Jim Rourke's disappearance, if he never returned, would probably join the hundreds of other riddles with which New Mexico abounded.

22

Hoping Without Praying

If Walt Bellamy's tale of those hoofprints was accurate, and Jim believed it was, then Halcón had chosen the old haunted Indian ruin for his residence.

Too, Halcón was very good at leaving sign for others to follow. Had he, then, deliberately left those tracks across the stage road, as he had left the dangling hangrope? As he had established that elaborate scheme to get Henry Drake to the mission graveyard?

The night was turning cold, which signified that a new day was only hours away from arriving.

Rourke halted when he thought he was about a mile from Anasazi Pueblo. He dismounted, buttoned his coat to the gullet, and wondered how close he had to be before Halcón would know he was out there.

He had to assume Halcón already knew.

Maybe he had known when Jim had left town.

From this point on the odds that he knew were against him began to increase. He could have turned back, except that he doubted that he would be able to make it. Halcón knew he was out there; Halcón rode a horse that Jim knew was tireless; his big horse could overtake Alex's mare long before Calabasas was in sight.

He ran clammy hands down the outside seam of his britches. The night was endlessly quiet, forebodingly so.

The roan mare picked grass at Jim's side, a reassuring condition. But Halcón would not be interested in the livery animal. Jim watched her anyway because horses, like dogs, could detect more by day or by night than people could.

She blissfully nipped curing grass heads.

He walked soundlessly in the direction of the broad, lower place where the old ruin endured moonlight as it had for perhaps a thousand years.

The mare dutifully responded to the tug on her lead rein. She only briefly pulled back once, when a small ground-owl exploded out of its underground burrow, frightened by the reverberation of something very heavy passing overhead.

Jim cursed and plunged his hand inside his

coat for the pistol. He was sweating; he was also concentrating so hard most of his senses were unusually keen.

When he thought he was close to one of the trails down into the wide arroyo, where moonlight would limn all the ancient square residences of a long-forgotten people, he was tempted to hobble the mare, take his Winchester, and scout ahead. The temptation passed. If Halcón was down there, and providing he had that unique sixth sense Father Cordero de la Cruz attributed to him, he knew Rourke was up there on the plateau above the ruins.

For the last time Rourke pondered the priest's admonition to let Halcón come to him, and right now it seemed like a good idea. Of course the priest had not meant for Rourke to hunt Halcón for a showdown, he had meant for Rourke to remain in town and wait.

Although Rourke had never liked that idea, right now he was willing to consider it because the moon was close to being full and if he went to the edge of the barranca the moonlight would outline him.

He hunkered in front of the roan mare. She, for her part, dozed. Jim had a clear view in all directions, but not for any great distance. A man with a carbine or a rifle would be able to bring Rourke into his sights from beyond the saloonman's visibility.

He arose and led the mare forward, the lead rein in his left hand, the Winchester in his right hand. The pistol gouged him under the coat. He had always been a good shot with a carbine or rifle, but he'd never been even passably accurate with a handgun.

It seemed to take hours for him to get close enough so that he could see down into the ruins, the creek-willows, and the tangle of tall grass and weeds along the creek bank.

He looked for the tall bay horse. Halcón could be concealed in a dozen places, but the big horse would require graze. Every horse that Rourke had ever seen required fodder of some kind at least twice a day, and in their natural state they grazed constantly.

He got down low, with the mare behind him, and made a particular point of studying the grassy verge alongside the creek for the horse. He must have been belly-down for close to half an hour before giving up.

There was no horse grazing beside the creek. Of course, he could be across the creek on the west side, in which case the willows that flourished on both sides of the watercourse would conceal him. Maybe not by daylight, but this was not daylight.

Rourke felt cold. If the horse was not there,

then neither was its rider. He wanted to derive satisfaction, even relief, from this notion, but instinct warned him. Attuned as he was, a simple hunch that he would have ignored in the past now had genuine significance.

He thought about calling to Halcón. That would, of course, confirm that he was out there and, perhaps more to the point, where he was out there.

Well, if Halcón was out there it was almost a certainty he knew who else was out there, and where he was.

And what would he say? This was a situation where words, a lot of them or a few of them, would be meaningless. Both he and Halcón knew why he was here.

If Halcón was as *coyote* as Father Cordero de la Cruz had implied, right now, near the rim above the ruin, Jim Rourke told himself his life had never before been, and probably would never again be, as close to fatal catastrophe.

He felt both fear and frustration increasing in his heart and mind as he lay peering down at the ghostly old ruins.

Rourke eased back, looked around at the placidly dozing roan mare, and wondered just how capable Halcón was. That he knew Rourke was here, Jim accepted. The plan he had devised last night hinged on something he did not know to be a fact, and was therefore something to worry about. It depended on just how much Halcón *did* know or was capable of surmising.

He went back to the mare, mounted, and turned southward; as he rode he figured the length of the reins to be looped around the saddlehorn so that the mare could not get her head down to eat. He made the reins snug, with just enough stretch for her to move well but without enough stretch for her to get her head down. He made two half hitches, mindful of the old adage that one half hitch would hold a bitch and two will hold the devil.

Another time he might have speculated on the origin of that remark. Right now he only made sure he had measured the reins correctly and made them secure; he lifted out his Winchester, rode several yards with it balanced across his lap, then, while the mare was hiking along, Rourke stepped off and slapped her on the rump with the carbine barrel.

She broke into a startled run, rattling small stones as she ran in the direction of town.

Rourke waited only long enough to be certain she was well on her way, then moved well west of where he had turned the mare loose, lost himself against the dark ground where grass and underbrush flourished, and waited.

His hope was that Halcón would believe Rourke had come hunting for him and had lost his nerve at the last moment and had fled back in the direction of Calabasas, and that Halcón would pursue him on the big, tireless bay horse to overtake and kill Rourke before he could reach safety.

It hinged on just how much Halcón was capable of, beyond his ability to know when he was being hunted.

Rourke knew very well that if the little priest knew and had failed to tell Jim that Halcón's sensing ability meant he knew a *man* was hunting him and would be guided by that knowledge instead of following a fleeing horse, then Jim Rourke had lost his struggle for survival. He was now afoot, miles from any settlement or ranch, and if Halcón already knew Rourke had tried to trick him, Jim Rourke's chances of survival were down to nothing.

He listened. The sound of the roan mare was rapidly diminishing. He swung in the other direction. There was no sound.

The chill increased to its predawn peak, but Rourke still sweated. As he lay, as tight wound as a spring, listening for the big bay horse, it occurred to him again that perhaps

Halcón had not been at Anasazi Pueblo after all, in which case Jim's situation was only slightly better. He would still have a long walk, no matter what direction he took. And — nothing would have been resolved. He would still be Halcón's target.

A motheaten coyote so old even his normally extraordinary sense of smell was blunted, came shambling along, watching with rheumy eyes for the first rodents of approaching dawn.

He passed within thirty feet of Rourke, never once raised his head to test for scents, never once looked either right or left. He had patches of shaggy hair, a scrawny, nearly hairless tail, and a gut so sunken he probably hadn't eaten in days.

It would have been merciful to shoot him. Rourke watched him pass without even thinking of shooting.

Seconds later his heartbeat quickened when he heard a loping horse coming from the direction of the ancient ruins. He had almost abandoned hope of hearing that sound.

A person did not have to be a horseman to appreciate the length of time between sounds of shod hooves rising and coming down again to know the horse hidden by distance and poor light had a very long stride. *Halcón had taken the bait!*

Rourke did not move. He would have risked a shot, but all he had was sound. Halcón had evidently struck out after the mare from the upper section of Anasazi Pueblo and was now riding straight, but at least one hundred yards east of where Rourke was lying.

Rourke had not expected this. His idea was that Halcón would leave the arroyo and follow directly in the mare's tracks. Rourke's idea had been to shoot Halcón out of the saddle when he came within range.

He lay listening to the big horse as long as sound was audible, then sat up, waited a moment before standing up, and listened intently in the direction of the big horse and heard nothing.

His best guess was that the big horse would overtake the roan mare before she had covered three miles, a period of time that should extend well past the oncoming sunrise.

Rourke's alternative to crossing endless empty miles in plain sight was Anasazi Pueblo. He hiked to the edge of the barranca, hesitated long enough to satisfy himself nothing was moving below, went down one of the paths to the arroyo's wide floor, made a straight line for the creek, shoved his way past willows, and dropped belly-down to drink. Sweat of any kind, but particularly a cold sweat, dehydrated a man.

He thought he had perhaps as much as two hours before Halcón returned. After leaning the carbine against a mud wall, he cut brush, went back up the trail, and walked back almost to where he had been lying before beginning to brush out his tracks.

When Halcón caught the riderless roan mare he would know exactly what had happened. He would return, looking for tracks. If there were none going down among the old ruins, he might spend time looking for them in other directions, but whatever Halcón did now, Rourke would be watching from just below the topmost rim of the barranca.

When the sun arose, visibility became perfect. The air was like glass, and the sky was a darker shade of blue than it would be after the sun had climbed, when it would become brassy and faded.

Rourke selected his place for spying from below the rim with care. He had plenty of time to do that. What bothered him now was Halcón's ability to sense when enemies were near. Would Halcón make it within carbine range before he sensed his enemy?

Rourke went back once more to fill up on water. As he got belly-down to drink, he had a distinct sensation of being watched. He rolled over, groping for the six-gun.

There was nothing; no movement, no sound, nothing but the forlorn ruins of mud buildings cramped together like the cells in a honeycomb.

He went back to his place just below the rim of the barranca, settled down with his carbine, and watched the sun-bright open plain. Several times, though, he whipped around to look back. He still saw nothing. As heat increased with no sighting of a rider, Rourke looked back several more times and still saw nothing.

He told himself that if he lived through this day wild horses couldn't drag him back to Anasazi Pueblo.

He no more believed in things a man could not see or touch than did anyone else. Nevertheless, this damned place made him distinctly uncomfortable. But it did not distract him from his purpose. Even the increasing heat as the morning wore along did not do that.

What *did* begin to worry him as the sun continued to climb and there was no sign of Halcón or anyone else on horseback was that Halcón was not going to return.

Why he had been in this place at all Rourke did not speculate about. He was only satisfied that Halcón had been here. With time passing he began to doubt very strongly that the coppery-hided man on the big bay horse would appear. He could imagine at least two good reasons for Halcón not to return; Rourke's appearance out here, and Rourke's successful ruse to draw Halcón out.

There could be reasons for Halcón to return that Rourke did not understand, but Rourke's arrival had spoiled the *barranca* as an isolated hiding place.

He did eventually see a rider, but the longer he watched, the less inclined he was to believe it was Halcón. For one thing the horse was not tall, for another, the rider slouched along, clearly bothered by the increasing heat.

He speculated; there had been the usual rumors of hoards of ancient gold buried out here, but as far as Rourke knew, they had been laughed out of existence long ago. This was not gold country. Nor were the prehistoric Indians interested in gold; their interests had been in water, game, plots of maize, and places to hide from other Indians.

Still, people occasionally came here to dig and pry, driving game away with their noise. They probably always would do these things. But no one in the Calabasas country came out here, except very rarely to gaze at what once had been, centuries before, a thriving Neolithic community — but never in the hottest time of the year.

Rourke sweated and watched the oncoming rider, silently cursing his approach because it could very well spook Halcón, if that was the right word.

By the time the sun had almost reached its meridian Rourke could identify the rider: Alex Jobey, the liveryman. That puzzled him even more. To his knowledge Alex rarely left town, even more rarely on horseback; he was addicted to the comfort of top buggies on the occasions when he had to leave town.

Alex hated heat. Rourke knew this better than most folks. Even when Alex had to hike the full length of town between his barn at the lower end and Rourke's saloon at the upper end, he walked on the shady side of the road. He had grumbled a dozen times in Jim's saloon that he hated New Mexico's summers.

The only reason Rourke could imagine for Alex to be coming out here was because the roan mare had not returned and he had tracked her in this direction. If that was so, then what in hell had happened to the roan mare?

He sat crouched until Alex was within shouting distance and had stopped to dismount and lead his horse toward the rim above Anasazi Pueblo.

The liveryman's shirt was soaked; his eyes

below the hatbrim were slits. He moved slowly, almost timidly, to the edge of the rim and looked down.

Rourke did not raise his voice when he said, "What the hell are you doing out here?"

Alex's jaw dropped, his slitted eyes popped wide open, the hand gripping the lead rein got white at the knuckles. He stood as stiff as a ramrod.

Rourke stood up to lean on his carbine. They stared at one another for seconds, then the liveryman reddened, clenched both hands into fists, and yelled. "Dang you, Jim Rourke, you liked to scairt the livin' daylights out of me."

Rourke remained silent until the other man regained a measure of self-control, then repeated the question. "What are you doin' out here?"

"What," exclaimed the angry liveryman, "are *you* doin' out here, an' where's my roan mare?"

Rourke gestured in the direction of willow shade at the creek. "Go tank up an' cool down."

"Where is my mare?"

"Alex, get down off the rim. Get down off the high ground."

"Why, dang you. Where is my — ?"

"Because if you stand up there like that,

there's a good chance you're goin' to get shot. Lead the damned horse down to the creek and water it. *Move, Alex!*"

The liveryman yanked at the horse and started down off the plateau. He said nothing until he looked back and saw Rourke hunkering just below the rim of the barranca.

He shook a fist at the saloonman's back. "You don't scare me one whit, Jim Rourke. Because of you an' whatever damned shenanigans you're up to, I can't find my roan mare."

His thirsty horse was pulling insistently toward the creek. The furious liveryman had to yield or be dragged.

Rourke ignored Jobey's grumbling profanity. The arrival of the irate liveryman had been a surprise, and was now also a cause for annoyance, but Jim Rourke's attention was on something far more critical — the return of Halcón and survival.

23

Through the Heart

The liveryman's arrival complicated things. Alex was noisy; he was known for grumbling, groaning and complaining, and right now his rancor seemed justified. He off-saddled his horse, left it on the far side of the creek, hobbled and happy, stalked up to where Rourke was squinting into the gelatinlike atmosphere of dancing heat, and rapped Jim on the arm. "What are you doing? Waiting for someone? Where is my roan mare?"

Rourke answered without looking around. "I set her loose last night — early this morning — with the reins looped so she couldn't get her head down to graze. The last I saw, she was hightailin' it toward town."

"Why did you turn her loose? Do you like to walk or are you crazy?"

Rourke's retort was delayed because in the shifting heat waves he thought he discerned a horseman. He was so far off he appeared to be about a foot or so off the ground, a common illusion during very hot weather.

Alex followed the line of Rourke's gaze, shook off sweat, and said, "I don't see nothin'."

Rourke ignored the liveryman. There definitely was an approaching rider coming from the south and angling westward toward Anasazi Pueblo.

Rourke raised his hat, mopped off sweat, tipped the hat far forward, and hunched lower to watch. Alex Jobey started to get to his feet in disgust.

Rourke grabbed the liveryman and forced him back down. Jobey exploded again. "Don't you manhandle me, you dang horsethief!"

Rourke stared at the other man. "I told you — don't get up in plain sight. Look south. You see him?"

Jobey squinted so hard his face contorted. When he pulled back he said, "Well, I see somethin'. What of it?"

"Alex, that's the feller who shot Jack Butts in the back, an' trapped Henry an' Ed into going where he was lying in wait to ambush them."

The liveryman's eyes widened. He turned for another gaze southward. "Who is he?"

"All I know is that he calls himself Halcón an' that he's a killer."

"An' he's comin' here, fer chris'sake?"

Rourke nodded and returned to watching the distant rider who sat straight-up in his saddle on the tall bay horse.

Jobey gripped Rourke's arm. "He's comin' here — why — what in hell is this?"

"He's comin' here to kill me, Alex. Go down to the creek an' stay there, an' be quiet."

The liveryman seemed to pale beneath his heat rash. He lingered a while as still as a stone while he stared at Jim Rourke. When he started to arise again Rourke growled without looking away from the oncoming horseman. "Down, damn it. Stay crouched until you reach the creek."

"Hell, he's better'n a mile away, Jim."

Rourke finally turned; he was angry. "Do what I say, because if he don't kill you, I will. Crouch and stay crouched. Now go on back to the creek an' stay there."

The liveryman left, moving crablike and bent nearly double. He did not straighten up until he was in willow shade, and there he burrowed past until he was within inches of the creek. He was thirsty, but he did not drink, not right away, just peered up from his willow screen at Jim Rourke crouching just below the rim. He only knew that Rourke was dead serious, and after what the saloonman had told him, Alex's sweat in his hiding place was cold. He was not heroic; horse-trading did not require courage, only shrewdness and a glib capacity to sound very virtuous while lying.

As Rourke watched the man approach, he saw Halcón halt, gazing at the ground. There was horse-sign out there but no sign of a man on foot, which Halcón probably thought there should be because when he had eventually overtaken the roan mare, she had been riderless.

Halcón may have thought the man he pursued heard him coming in the predawn darkness and had left the animal to seek a hiding place.

He had let the roan mare continue on toward Calabasas after releasing the looped lines, not out of any feeling for the horse wanting to graze, but because he did not want the mare to reach Calabasas until he got back to Anasazi Pueblo.

He had not bothered to do much sign reading. He did not have to: in these circumstances he relied entirely on a very powerful otherworldly instinct which had never failed him.

He thought indifferently that the saloonman had left the roan farther south, but after freeing her and facing toward Anasazi Pueblo he knew exactly where to find his man.

As Rourke watched, Halcón resumed his approach. He rode slowly, peering intently ahead. He took no evasive action, which only half surprised Jim Rourke, who had hair standing straight up on the back of his neck. His heart was pounding; he could hear its echoes in his head.

Halcón finally changed course; he rode north out of carbine range and continued on that course until Rourke had to expose his upper body to see him. Finally, well north of Anasazi Pueblo, Halcón took a downward path into the canyon, which was where Rourke lost sight of him.

Now the saloonman was as close to panic as he had ever been in his life. His perch below the barranca was no longer protective; in fact, when Halcón came down the canyon, probably on foot, he would be behind Rourke.

Jim prayed hard that he would be able to reach the ruins before the killer got down that far. He moved swiftly, watching the upper end of the canyon as he got among the crumbly old earthen walls that were nowhere higher than a man's waist, and squatted with both hands sweat-slippery on the carbine.

Across from him were the dense willows

where Alex had gone. Across from Alex on the far side of the creek, Rourke could hear the liveryman's horse stamping at gnats as he cropped grass. Those were the only sounds.

Rourke's nerves were taut; sweat ran into his eyes. He wiped it off with a filthy cuff and strained to hear sound coming from up the canyon.

It was a long time before he heard it, but when it was eventually audible, Rourke wiped both palms on his britches and regripped the carbine. To Rourke's knowledge, there were three men down there, and only one of them had gone north before entering the canyon.

He did not see the coppery-skinned man for nearly a quarter of an hour after he heard him approaching, and when he raised his head with just his eyes showing, Halcón was taking his time. He seemed to be functioning as bird dogs functioned, by moving ahead slowly, making sure he was walking in the proper direction, which he was, but the slowness had Jim Rourke sweating rivers and scarcely breathing as he estimated distances. He would have one chance, one shot. He was absolutely convinced he would be allowed to get off just one shot.

Halcón was not carrying his Winchester. His sidearm had the tie-down hanging loose, something killers did when they anticipated the need for a fast draw.

The distance between where Rourke was crouching and the creek willows was roughly forty or fifty feet. Rourke had Halcón in carbine range. He shuffled slightly behind his mud wall so he could lie flat and shoot upward when they came face to face.

If Rourke had any advantage it might be that when Halcón whirled to face him, he would not be looking down; that two-second advantage could be the determining factor in their shootout.

It certainly was not much to rely on, but Rourke had nothing else; there was no place and it was too late to run.

Halcón was well within carbine range, but slightly north of Rourke's hiding place when he halted, cocked his head, stood a moment, then laughed as he began moving — toward Alex's hiding place among the willows.

Rourke held his breath as Halcón came into view facing the willows, his back to Rourke. Halcón drew his six-gun without haste.

Rourke settled both elbows against the ground, tipped the carbine up, centered it on Halcón's back, and was squeezing the trigger when Halcón suddenly whirled.

The muzzleblast was very loud. The bullet hit Halcón squarely through the heart. He had one second to show disbelief before he fell.

Alex was whimpering in his hiding place. Rourke did not arise, he was watching something he never would have believed if he hadn't seen it with his own eyes.

Halcón's head turned very slowly; he searched the area behind him with slow sweeps of both eyes. As Rourke watched, the eyes stopped moving, seemed to shrink, then disappeared.

Rourke forgot everything but what he had done and its aftermath. It occurred to him only very belatedly that Halcón's instinct had functioned exactly as it was supposed to, but instead of stalking one man, Halcón had stalked two men. Only at the last moment had he evidently understood that he was following the wrong sense, which was when he had whirled and the bullet intended for the middle of his back struck him in the heart.

Rourke did not move for half an hour, by which time the sun was on its downward curve. When he finally arose, he walked ahead, poked at the corpse with the barrel of his carbine, felt how very light it had become, turned it face up, but only very briefly before turning it face down again.

Halcón was older in the body now, but not very much older, and he was dehydrated as though whatever had been freed from the body when death came had taken moisture with it along with the eyes.

Rourke stood looking down, remembering the *other thing* Father Cordero de la Cruz said occurred when these things ended, but made no move to verify that, he would leave that to the buzzards to verify. He went plunging through the willows to find Alex.

The liveryman was lying half in the creek. Rourke pulled him out of the water and dropped to one knee. Jobey was breathing but unconscious. His face was the color of putty.

Rourke turned aside to drink deeply. Within moments fresh sweat broke out over his body. He looked for Alex's horse and found it dozing, occasionally flicking its tail, hip-shot and completely relaxed. If it had heard the gunshot it had made a rapid recovery from being startled.

It was not a young animal. It was the kind for which life held few surprises and none worth losing rest or grazing over.

Rourke saddled and bridled it, splashed it back across the creek, left it beside its unconscious owner, and returned to the dehydrated corpse to retrieve Halcón's six-gun. There was nothing in his pockets but a sizable amount of paper money, which Rourke left.

He hoisted Alex across the seat of the saddle, led the horse out to clear ground, mounted behind the cantle, and reined the animal toward one of the paths leading up out of Anasazi Pueblo.

It was a long, plodding, uncomfortable ride back to town. They did not reach there until long after dark, with Alex only beginning to groan and feebly struggle as they approached the outskirts.

Rourke balanced the liveryman in the saddle from the ground, made sure he would not fall, and headed the horse toward the livery barn at the lower end of town. The few people who saw Alex pass probably thought he was drunk.

Rourke entered his saloon from the back alley. It was not too late for customers to arrive if he lighted a lamp and unbarred the roadway door. But he did not do these things.

He should have been hungry, but wasn't. He drank water, washed in cold water, had a jolt of whiskey, and went out front to sit a while on the backbar stool. He felt drained; even walking was difficult. If he had looked at his reflection in the backbar mirror, he would have been shocked.

The jolt of whiskey restored him, at least for the time being. He tossed his coat atop the canvas pallet in the storeroom, left again by the back alley doorway, walked steadily down through Mex-town to the mission, and used the butt of Halcón's six-gun to hammer on a door.

It was a while before the priest arrived, candle held high. He stepped back, but Rourke shook his head and led the way to the old bench where they had sat before. Father Cordero de la Cruz blew out the candle; there was a paling horizon far to the east.

Rourke held out Halcón's Colt butt first. The priest looked at the weapon, but made no move to take it. *"Las suyas?"*

"Yes."

"You are very tired, companion. We can talk tomorrow."

Rourke made a small, mirthless smile. "Tomorrow, Father, I will sleep the clock around — then sleep some more. You were right — he had some kind of way to know where I was . . . but when we met, the liveryman was about forty feet in the opposite direction. Halcón's instinct or whatever it was evidently was not capable of a very close identification. This I don't know. I thought about it on the ride back. Maybe he heard the liveryman's horse eating grass across the creek. He stopped facing in that direction — with this gun in his hand.

"I got flat down and aimed for his back between his shoulders. Something made him whirl as I was pulling the trigger . . . Here, keep his gun. It may have significance to you. To me — I only want to get rid of it. The bullet struck him in the heart."

"You left — ?"

"Father, he was dead. No man lives even moments when he is shot through the heart. I can tell you what happened . . . Father, the eyes disappeared from the sockets. The liveryman fainted. I brought him back to town across his saddle. Now I have one question — will he return?"

Father Cordero de la Cruz sat back in silence, shaking his head. After a while he said, "No. He has many other places to go. One failure out of thousands of successes is nothing to him. Even now he has already appeared in another place — somewhere." The priest took the pistol, gazed at it in his lap for a moment, then stood up. "Go home, companion, rest, sleep, open your saloon, become normal again. You and I will share some wine when the afternoons are cooler someday — and talk."

Rourke arose. "Something else I thought about on the ride back — If his instinct failed him this time, if it caused him to be killed . . . why did that happen? You said he knew when an enemy was coming . . ."

The priest arose, brushed Rourke's arm with a hand, and smiled. "You see, my friend . . . this is one of the things we will discuss someday when it is cool. Good night."

Rourke returned to the saloon, fell asleep atop the folds of canvas, and did not awaken until the following afternoon.

He opened the saloon for his nightly regulars, but met their inquisitive stares with a smile and silence. Even when Slade Downing arrived, Rourke served him, told Downing he had overslept, and added nothing to that statement.

Life in Calabasas, a frontier community, was accustomed to delays, surprises, even little riddles, accepted as part of life. Three days later, with the saloon operating again at its normal schedule, Rourke's absence was already beginning to fade in people's minds.

Only one thing occurred, on the fourth day. The old grizzled cowman who had feared his wife's iron skillet walked in, looking pleased with himself, and told Jim Rourke a tale the saloonman understood perfectly; certainly better than the old rancher did.

"I bought the livery barn off'n Alex. What d'you think of that?"

Rourke nodded without speaking.

The cowman signaled for a bottle and a

glass. As Rourke went to get those items the cowman leaned down on the bar and smiled at his reflection in the backbar mirror.

"I never figured Alex would sell. He had a real good business . . . I made him an offer an' he took it without no haggling. But I had to ask why'n hell he would sell, an' what he said didn't make a lick of sense."

"What did he say?"

"Well — somethin' about when a man hears that laugh twice, it's time for him to get as far away as he can because sure as hell if he ever hears it again . . . That's all he said.

"One thing. He insisted on takin' a roan mare with him, everything else was mine. Care to drink to the new town liveryman, Jim?"

Rourke drank, refused payment, and after the cowman departed, Rourke cared for his other customers without saying a word, only smiling and nodding.

We hope you have enjoyed this Large Print book. Other Thorndike Press or Chivers Press Large Print books are available at your library or directly from the publishers. For more information about current and upcoming titles, please call or write, without obligation, to:

Thorndike Press
P.O. Box 159
Thorndike, Maine 04986
USA
Tel. (800) 223-6121 (U.S. & Canada)
In Maine call collect: (207) 948-2962

OR

Chivers Press Limited
Windsor Bridge Road
Bath BA2 3AX
England
Tel. (0225) 335336

All our Large Print titles are designed for easy reading, and all our books are made to last.